E.J. RUSSELL

BEST
BEAST

AN ENCHANTED OCCASIONS STORY

Best Beast

Cover concept by Natasha Snow Designs, http:// natashasnow.com
Edited by Meg DesCamp

ISBN: 978-1-947033-27-6

First edition
January, 2021

Contact information:
ejr@ejrussell.com

E.J. RUSSELL

BEST
BEAST

AN ENCHANTED OCCASIONS STORY

Author's Note

When I wrote *Nudging Fate* and later *Devouring Flame*, I imagined the Olesson-Pakulski wedding, the event that tanked Enchanted Occasions' reputation, as akin to Sherlock Holmes's offhand comment about the giant rat of Sumatra: "a story for which the world is not yet prepared."

But then I started to wonder...

YOU'RE INVITED

Radka Miroslava Pakulski
and
Ole Storstrand Olesson
invite you to join them at the celebration of their wedding
on Imbolc
at one thirty in the afternoon
at the Oslo Interstices

*Gluten-free, non-GMO Interstitial adaptation elixir will be
provided for all guests; please RSVP with any known herring
allergies*

CHAPTER ONE

If he lived to be three thousand and two, Jovan Kos would never understand why his best friend agreed to hold his bachelor party in the Las Vegas Interstices. Sure, it was the last day of January, and the Interstices—the post-creation gaps between realms—didn't *completely* reflect the weather in their Earthside counterparts, but Las Vegas was in the freaking desert, for fuck's sake. Ole's frost goblin clan hailed from Niflheim, a realm that was nothing but wall-to-wall ice, snow, and mist. With his thick full-body fur, Ole had to be miserable in this heat. Jovan wasn't that comfortable himself, his dress shirt sticking to his skin, and he was human. Ish. Most of the time.

But Ole had given Jovan the sad-puppy eyes and said that Radka, his bride-to-be, was having her bachelorette party here too, and one peculiar feature of Radka's vila culture required the bridesmaids to kidnap the groom midway through the festivities.

Whatever.

So as Ole's best man, Jovan had caved, coordinated with Radka's snooty maid of honor to set it up, and booked this bar for the party's exclusive use.

Something had to be wrong with the environmental spells though, because the place could double as the antechamber of Muspelheim, the Norse fire realm. He glowered at the bartender, who'd come to refresh his drink. "What's with the air conditioning?" The faun bartender gulped and inched back, his goatee quivering and his hooves *tip-tip-tipp*ing on the wooden floor. *Fuck. Better tone down the attitude.* Because Jovan really needed that drink. "Sorry." He tapped the rim of his highball glass with one finger. "Same again, please."

The bartender nodded, snatched the empty with the tips of his fingers, keeping as far away from Jovan as possible, and practically sprinted back to the other end of the bar. Jovan sighed and tugged at his shirt collar, hoping in vain for a little breeze.

A shriek split the air and Jovan leaped off his barstool, sending it crashing to the floor. He reached for his sidearm and came up empty. Loki's balls, why had he agreed to surrender his weapon at the intergate? The bartender was crouched behind the bar, his arms over his head, clearly not about to stage an intervention.

Fuck it. Armed or not, Jovan was fully capable of countering most threats. His inner wolf warrior was never far below the surface, but he loosened his iron control, allowing heat to build behind his eyes as he crept forward until he could see past the pony wall that separated the bridal party from the rest of the empty bar.

Radka and her bridesmaids were fluttering around like so many blonde sparrows, while a wizened old woman dressed head to toe in rusty black—including her babushka—rocked in her seat with a very poorly knitted shawl thrown over her head.

Poor Ole sat at the other side of the oval table with an even more poorly knitted hat jammed on his head and draped in at least three mufflers. He was clutching a tall glass of ice almost desperately, and his big paws were encased in heavy mittens.

What the fuck? The man could weather sub-zero temperatures naked. Why the Hel did he need ratty winter gear in a bar that was three degrees away from a sauna?

Jovan wasn't supposed to intervene in this part of the proceedings—his job was technically done once the bridesmaids had "kidnapped" Ole from the very sedate poker game that was all Ole would allow for his bachelor party. But Jovan wasn't leaving until he was sure Ole hadn't melted into a fricking puddle.

Besides, Jovan felt a personal responsibility for making sure this weekend ran smoothly. Not only was he Ole's best man, he was the one who'd introduced him to Radka. At the time, he'd never seen this relationship coming. Nobody had. Who'd have believed that a frost goblin and a vila would ever fall in love?

Jovan hesitated, debating whether to wade in and demand explanations. The only thing that stopped him was that Ole didn't look distressed. *If you don't count incipient heat prostration.* Instead, he was gazing at Radka with that same dreamy half-smile on his face he'd worn since the day Radka had proposed to him.

Jovan shook his head. "What the fuck is all the fuss about?" he muttered.

A cool breeze wafted across his neck and a low, husky voice, its tone laced with buried laugher, murmured, *"Propuh,"* from the space on his left.

Jovan smiled in spite of himself. "Kai. Who the Hel is *Propuh* to cause this kind of stir? A gremlin? An ifrit? A Mongolian death worm?"

A chuckle rose from the empty air. "*Propuh* isn't a who, Jovan. It's a what."

"Don't keep me in suspense. I've faced down hundreds of supernatural and magical menaces, but this is a new one. What kind of weapon do I need? Should I call for backup?"

The old woman continued to shriek as she tottered out of her chair and hefted a giant carpet bag onto the table. She pulled out another ratty muffler and tried to wrap it around Radka's neck. Radka rolled her blue eyes, unwound it and stuffed it back in the bag, but the old woman yanked it out again and tried to enswathe one of the bridesmaids. Jovan couldn't tell which one—they all looked alike to him except for Taline, the maid of honor, whose eyes were nearly black instead of blue.

An invisible hand patted his arm. "It's a false alarm anyway, my friend. And entirely my fault."

Not for the first time, Jovan wished he could see Kai Schiffer in the flesh. He knew, from where Kai's voice emanated, that the man was about five-ten, a good eight inches shorter than Jovan himself. He knew that Kai used cologne or body wash that smelled of a fresh ocean breeze. He knew that Kai's dry humor came closer to making him laugh than anything in the multiverse, and that Kai's voice always made him half hard.

But he'd never seen his face. Or any part of his body, for that matter.

Kai was a HAH—a half-and-half, aka aitcher, someone who was a mixture of human and one or more supernatural races. In Kai's case, his supernatural half was Klabautermann, a relatively rare race who lived invisibly aboard ships, only becoming visible when the boat they were committed to was about to sink. His human half allowed him to live Earthside, but whenever he entered the Interstices—which was the only place Jovan had ever spent time with him—his Klabautermann side activated and he turned invisible.

Damn it.

"Don't hold out on me, Kai. Did you bring this *propuh* in with you?"

"Weeelll," Kai drawled. "In a way, but you can stand down, Agent Kos. *Propuh* is a draft."

Jovan blinked. "A draft? You mean like moving air?"

"Exactly. Where Radka's family is from, *propuh* is feared more than, oh"—Kai's tone turned teasing—"a grumpy, six-foot-six Interstitial Law Enforcement agent. Who just *might* go into wolf berserker mode when the inclination strikes."

"Let me get this straight." Jovan glared at the spot where he'd triangulated Kai's eyes to be. "They're afraid of the *air*? No wonder this place is hermetically sealed."

Kai's warm chuckle zinged straight to Jovan's balls. "Did you think this establishment went to the trouble of reversing their environmental spells just for fun? That poor bartender is sweating bullets."

Jovan rubbed the back of his neck. "That, uh, may be my fault. I might have intimidated him a little bit."

"You? Intimidating? Jovan, you shock me." Kai's hand slid between Jovan's arm and his side, and Jovan automatically bent his elbow so Kai could rest his hand there. "This particular instance of *propuh* is entirely my doing. I was in the men's room and passed a little too close to Baba Lenka on my way to join you."

Jovan's own laugh was rusty as Hel. *When did I laugh last?* Probably the last time he was with Kai, at that little restaurant in the Oslo Interstices when Ole and Radka had announced their engagement. "Do you suppose you could run back and forth behind Ole for a while? The poor guy could use a little *propuh*."

"Are you kidding?" Kai pulled Jovan toward the bar, and Jovan let himself be pulled—which never happened with anybody except Kai. "Baba Lenka would force more of her horrible knitwear on him and he'd probably pass out, which Baba Lenka would take as the worst possible omen, I'm sure. And trust me, I don't want anything to interfere with this wedding. Or anything *more*," he muttered.

"What's that supposed to mean?"

Kai's sigh was clearly audible, even over the continued clamor from the bachelorettes—plus one overheated goblin and one delusional baba. "Later. First, I need a drink, and, for obvious reasons, it's impossible for me to attract the bartender's attention."

"Fine." Jovan submitted to Kai's tugs and resumed stalking toward the cowering bartender. "But only because I need something too. An extremely tall something. Or an ice bath."

"Really?" Kai's tone held interest now. "I didn't think you Jötnar were so susceptible to heat, not like the frost goblins. You're not furred or scaled." A finger traced a line across Jovan's cheek, making him shiver despite the tropical temperature. "Your skin doesn't feel any different from mine." The touch vanished. *Damn it.* "Sorry. That was inappropriate. I should have asked first."

Jovan swallowed. "I don't mind." *What I wouldn't give to touch his skin.* Although first he'd have to find it. "A Jötunn can be many things." He snorted. "Consider my half siblings, if you don't believe me."

"Yes. A wolf, a snake, and the woman who may or may not be half-corpse. I always wondered how you managed to turn out so human-looking."

"It helps that Loki wasn't my father." Jovan's father had been human—but that wasn't something he could ever reveal, even to Kai. In Jovan, the DNA combination of his Jötunn mother and his human father had produced a Úlfheðinn, a wolf warrior and sometime berserker. *A beast.* "Even though I lack Ole's heavy pelt, I'm stationed in the Stockholm Interstices. We're not used to sweltering." They reached the bar and Jovan pulled out a stool for Kai, then sat on the stool to his right with a clear view of the table, earning a side-eye from the bartender. Jovan ignored him. "What'll you have?"

The bartender's eyes widened, and he looked about ready to bolt. "I...er..."

"Stop terrorizing the poor man, Jovan. I'll have a bottle of Mountain King red ale, please." A knock sounded on the bar in front of Jovan. "And a bucket of ice for my friend to soak his head in."

Jovan glanced sidelong in Kai's direction as the bartender scuttled away in a clatter of hooves. "Everybody else in the multiverse cuts a wide swath around me." *Which is just the way I like it.* "But not you. Why?"

"I'm the executive assistant for the general manager of a television studio. She makes you look like a fluffy kitten."

Jovan lifted an eyebrow. "What does an executive assistant do?"

"Make life easier for the GM. If I do my job right, nobody even knows I'm there."

"In other words—"

"Like any good Klabautermann, I'm invisible except when doom looms." His tone was wry. "When I'm conveniently there to take the blame."

My stars, could I sound any more pathetic? Kai snagged a bar mat and pulled it toward himself. Manipulating some kind of prop that others could see made his Interstitial invisibility easier to manage—for others, anyway. As long as he didn't pick the object up fully and catch it in his transparency matrix, it gave them a reference point.

Jovan, though, had never treated Kai as *nothing*. Even during their first meeting two years ago, when Radka had dragged him to an Interstitial club so Kai could meet her new boyfriend, Jovan had always behaved as if Kai were as visible here as he was Earthside. Kai had often wished that there had been some way for them to meet face to face. *And maybe body to body?*

But Jovan was a Pure, and they didn't do well outside their home realms. To spend time in the Interstices or in foreign realms, including Earthside, they had to take special adaptation elixirs, which could have serious side effects over time. Kai had heard that ILE agents had special spell implants, like Earthside nicotine patches, so they could move from realm to realm at will in pursuit of criminals.

But that same rumor stated that since the ILE was forbidden from interfering Earthside, their implants prevented them from crossing the threshold.

Kai sighed. Attempting a hookup while invisible was a logistical nightmare. His gaze slid to Jovan's profile—his strong jaw dusted with sexy dark scruff, his blade of a nose, his deep-set eyes the color of onyx. *For him, I'd make the effort.* But would Jovan be willing to put up with the hassle? Sure they were friends, but given Kai's lack of visible body parts whenever they'd met, it was like perpetual online dating with no hope of an IRL meetup. *Hell, I could flash my dick right now, and nobody would ever know.*

Not that he would risk it. Traditionally, Klabautermänner were only visible to their boat's crew and passengers who were about to die. His own father had been shunned by his clan and forbidden to ever take ship again when he'd fallen in love with Kai's mother and rescued her from the wreck.

Jovan's job was perilous enough already. Some supernatural races were plenty scary when they *weren't* criminals—wendigos sprung to mind—and Kai didn't want to tempt fate by adding a Klabautermann sighting to Jovan's danger quotient.

The bartender returned with Kai's ale and a highball glass full of a pale amber liquid and clinking with ice. "Did you..." He licked parched lips, the horns protruding from his shaggy brown hair quivering. "Were you serious about the ice bucket?"

Jovan just glared, but Kai laughed. "You don't need to bother." He nudged Jovan with his elbow, earning him one of those delicious growls. "Although maybe later." He flicked a fingernail against Jovan's glass with a soft *tink.* "What are you drinking? Scotch rocks?"

"Ginger ale." Jovan's scowl deepened at Kai's laugh and he curled the long fingers of one of his big square hands around his glass. "I don't drink when I'm on duty."

"You're his best man, not his bodyguard."

Jovan cast a dark glance at the table where Baba Lenka was wrapping yet another scarf around poor Ole's neck. "Seems like he needs a bodyguard at the moment."

"Not a bodyguard, although he may need intravenous fluids before the ceremony tomorrow."

Kai took a swig of his beer, causing the bartender's eyes to pop when the bottle disappeared and then reappeared when Kai set it down. Stars and storms, this was the *Interstices.* The silly man should be inured to the unusual by now. This whole bar was nothing more than a freaking magical construct.

Jovan turned, his gaze focusing unerringly on where Kai's face was. "Didn't Ole and Radka hire that fancy event planning agency to run this circus?"

"Enchanted Occasions, yes." Kai smiled crookedly. "Its owner and all its staff are aitchers. Radka insisted on booking them as a nod to me, despite some pretty extreme opposition from her entire extended family. Although I think she took a certain smug satisfaction out of besting them in the melee. They're still on her case about divorcing her first husband, let alone marrying a goblin."

"If this outfit is so good, why did they stage the bachelorette party in this dump?" Jovan lifted his glass at the bartender. "No offense."

"They didn't. The maid of honor is one of the javerzaharses."

"The what now?"

"Armenian nymphs. Aka, the 'perpetual brides.' Their species exists literally to plan weddings, and she was certain Radka would let her wrangle this one, even though she was one of the most vocal in her objections to Ole." Kai took another long pull of ale. "Imagine her surprise when Radka didn't take her up on her ever-so-kind offer."

"Fireworks?"

"You have no idea. Radka allowed her to be in charge of the bachelorette party to preserve the peace. More or less."

Jovan glanced over his shoulder at the party. "Why aren't you hanging out with them, anyway? You're Radka's best friend. For that matter, why is that Taline witch the maid of honor? Radka's not exactly a traditional vila. I'd have thought she'd insist on you as her man of honor, tradition be damned."

Kai rolled his eyes, which lost a lot of impact considering Jovan couldn't see him do it. "Jovan, the wedding is in the Oslo Interstices. The *Interstices.*"

"Yeah. So?"

"So imagine having an empty space in all the wedding photos. Or an arm's-length gap between Radka and the next bridesmaid while they're standing at the altar."

"Hmmm. I guess that would be awkward."

"You think?" He took another gulp. "Radka and Ole are putting up with enough from both families. They didn't need what would look like a political statement on top of everything."

"Don't the event planners have a magical doohickey that could make you visible for the festivities? They offered me one to let me go Earthside."

Excited butterflies caromed around Kai's ribcage. *You don't say. Let's get back to that later.* "Think about it. Everybody in Radka's family knows about me. They know what I am. If you think Baba Lenka had a fit about *propuh*, imagine what would happen with an actual Klabautermann sighting."

Jovan winced. "Right. That could get ugly."

"No kidding. Baba Lenka is already prophesying doom because this is Radka's second wedding. She's demanding all kinds of concessions to ward off bad luck."

"What kind of concessions?"

Kai chuckled, even though it wasn't the least bit funny. "You know how usually the wedding ceremony is followed by a cocktail hour and then a reception?"

"Of course."

"Baba Lenka demanded that the ceremony come *last.*"

Jovan's brows drew together further. "What the— Why? And who the Hel is Baba Lenka, anyway?"

"She's Radka's maternal grandmother." Kai shrugged. "And she claims that inverting the ceremony order will confuse any entity with an evil agenda—although she didn't specify who that might be—and prevent even more bad luck."

"If you asked me," Jovan growled as Baba Lenka, wailing in Serbian, tried to wrestle a scarf around Radka's neck again, over her daisy-print sundress, "Baba Lenka brought the bad luck with her." His glare ought to have set her headscarf on fire. "Ole never mentioned this old bat to me before. Do they keep her locked in an attic somewhere most of the time?"

"Hardly." Kai swiveled his stool to lean his back against the bar and observe the table. "She's the CEO of their family's wind turbine business."

Jovan's jaw sagged. "She's what? Then why does she look like a refugee from a bad Russian folktale?"

"Shhh!" Kai clapped his hand over Jovan's mouth. Jovan's eyes widened, but then they crinkled at the corners and his mouth moved against Kai's palm, and since Kai was invisible, he could see exactly how devastating the curve of those lips was. *Gods, that smile.* Kai dropped his hand before he lost his mind and traced Jovan's lips. "Never let her hear you say that. She's Serbian, not Russian."

"I don't care if she's the lost princess of Atlantis, if she puts one more scarf around Ole's neck, I'm taking her down."

"Not the best way to ingratiate yourself with Radka's family, Mr. Best Man."

"Ask me if I care."

CHAPTER TWO

Kai's chuckle diverted Jovan's attention from the table. "You don't mean that. You'd never hurt anyone smaller than yourself. Not unless it was part of your job."

"I told you. Taking care of Ole *is* my job for the next two days." Jovan downed half his ginger ale, the bubbles tickling his nose and the ice cubes nudging his lips with welcome coolness. "What's Radka's family's beef with Ole, anyway? You couldn't meet a nicer guy. He's smart. He's got more money than Loki—"

Kai snorted. "Bet that frosts Loki's balls."

Jovan was surprised into his own rusty chuckle. "You have no idea." He slanted a glance at Kai's head-space. "Everyone around Radka objects to Ole except you. Why is that?"

The magical disappearing beer bottle blinked into view on the bar with a thump. "Probably because I'm the only one who cares about Radka herself"—Kai's voice held a steely edge—"and not about tradition or social status or things that *simply aren't done*." He squeezed Jovan's arm, causing his sleeve to crumple with the outline of Kai's fingers. "I can never be grateful enough to you for introducing her to Ole. He's the best thing that's ever happened to her, and I'm willing to do anything, put up with anything, including getting railroaded out of the wedding party and being treated like the forerunner of the apocalypse by Baba Lenka, if it means Radka and Ole get married tomorrow and escape all the drama."

Jovan swallowed. *Does he mean he'd do* me? *If I asked—* But he resolutely pushed the notion away. He had the same goal for this weekend as Kai: Make sure that Ole and Radka's wedding went off without a hitch so they could honeymoon far away from their interfering families. Although Ole's family, as far as Jovan had been able to determine, was less poisonous than Radka's. As long as you didn't count Ole's Uncle Snorre. And Uncle Snorre wasn't strictly poisonous—he was a sweet, absent-minded goblin who just happened to be...slightly undead.

Greatly daring, Jovan let his hand hover above those telltale sleeve creases, lowering it until, with a good inch of airspace between his shirt and his palm, he could feel Kai's skin. Was that a hitch in Kai's breath? Was his hand trembling just a bit? "Then the two of us have the same goal. Make sure our friends come out the other side happily married and launched into their new lives." He glanced at the table where Baba Lenka was extracting another improbably long muffler from her carpet bag. "Without bonus knitwear."

Kai's laughter this time was a little shaky. "Agreed. Shall we make a pact?"

"I think we just did."

"Not yet. We just agreed to the terms. To formalize it, I, Kai Schiffer, pledge to do everything in my power to make sure our friends get married tomorrow and embark on their happy ever after. Knitwear optional." Kai nudged

Jovan's shoulder. "After all, Ole does live in Niflheim. Cozy outerwear might be necessary."

"Not that kind." He glowered as Baba Lenka approached Ole with yards of rainbow striped scarf. Before she reached her target, Radka took her elbow and steered her away, removing the scarf from Baba Lenka's hands and looping it around her own neck. It didn't exactly complement her sundress, but the glance of affectionate apology she shot Ole made it look like haute couture. *Yeah, Ole deserves that kind of love. So does she.* "I, Jovan Kos, pledge to— Wait." Jovan half stood, dislodging Kai's hand from his arm, because the blonde bridesmaid flock was surrounding Ole and pulling him out of his chair. "What's going on?" Jovan lunged forward, but Kai caught his arm in a surprisingly strong grip.

"They're kidnapping him, of course. You knew about that."

"But—" Jovan tracked the women leading Ole toward the bar's entrance. None of them came up higher than his armpit, but somehow they struck Jovan as sinister anyway —perky giggliness notwithstanding. "They already kidnapped him. From the bachelor party poker game an hour ago. That's why he's here."

"That was just the beginning." Kai's sigh gusted along Jovan's jaw. "They have to separate him from Radka now." Sure enough, Radka was still at the table with Baba Lenka. "This'll be the hardest part for both of them. Together they can withstand everybody. Separately? More of a challenge."

"But—"

"Count Ole lucky that Baba Lenka didn't go with the bridesmaids." He sighed again. "Unfortunately, that means Radka is stuck with her, and without Ole for backup, I'm afraid of what she'll cave to. If you'll excuse me for a minute? I want to see if she needs me."

The waft of cool air scented with ocean wasn't necessary for Jovan to know Kai was gone from his side. He could tell, because that electric tingle, that *awareness* of Kai vanished. He sat down heavily and signaled the bartender. "Same again."

✦

Kai glanced back at Jovan. He wasn't sure Jovan wouldn't take off after Ole and the bridesmaids, tailing them with an ILE agent's stealth and a Úlfheðinn's single-minded ferocity. If something happened to disrupt the planned events, Radka's family could very well use it as leverage to stop the wedding. But Jovan had resumed his seat at the bar, so that bullet was successfully dodged.

He approached the table littered with empty glasses, their festive paper umbrellas somehow forlorn amid the melting ice. For a wonder, Baba Lenka was simply sitting straight-backed in her chair with her carpetbag in her lap instead of haranguing Radka about undutiful children or bad omens or disappointing quarterly profits. Somehow, Baba Lenka could conflate tradition, superstition, and corporate strategy into a weapon that zinged straight through Radka's defenses.

Family. What can you do? Kai was grateful for a change that he had only his parents to worry about, given that his father's Klabautermann clan had washed their hands of him, and his mother's family had all perished in the shipwreck.

Kai triangulated the best way to reach Radka without passing too close to Baba Lenka and initiating another *propuh* meltdown. He edged his way around the table, sticking as close as possible to the pony walls that surrounded it. The chair next to Radka had been pulled away from the table during the bridesmaids' precipitous exit with the hapless groom, so Kai was able to sit down without moving it.

Baba Lenka also objected to invisible best friends. Go figure.

"Hey," he murmured, taking care to keep his voice lower than the seventies' disco mix piping through the bar's sound system. "You need some company? I'll hang out with you if you want."

She shook her head imperceptibly, her long blond hair drifting against Kai's arm below the sleeve of his T-shirt. She took her cell phone out of her canary yellow clutch and pretended to answer a call. It earned her a huff from Baba Lenka, who pointedly turned her back. Taking calls at family events was one of her pet peeves, but she also had a deep respect for confidential business communication. The only way Kai and Radka could speak in her presence was if Radka pretended to take a job-related call.

"Radka Pakulski," she said, keeping her tone businesslike to preserve the fiction. "One moment, please." She turned to Baba Lenka. "I'm sorry, Baba, but I must take this. It's the station."

Baba Lenka waved one hand, although she didn't turn around. "Go, go. Think nothing of me. I am of no importance."

Radka rolled her eyes, but stood and rounded the table, taking the same path Kai had. He followed her until they were a safe distance away, halfway between the table and the bar.

She turned and faced him. She always knew where he was. Something in her vila nature—probably the same thing that had made her an excellent meteorologist at the TV station where they both worked—gave her a practical affinity for air currents that had either escaped the rest of her family or else they chose to ignore it in favor of *propuh*. "If I get through this weekend without visiting the biggest cyclone this side of Kansas on my family, it will be a miracle."

Kai chuckled and took her hands. "You wouldn't. Think of the special reports you'd have to log on the storm."

"Not my job anymore." She winced at Kai's flinch. "Sorry. But the new job—"

"I know. An offer you couldn't refuse, not to mention much more convenient to your new home with Ole. I'm happy for you, even though I'll miss you."

"I'll miss you too. You've kept me grounded the last few weeks through all the wedding bullshit." She sighed with a fleeting glance at Baba Lenka's ramrod straight spine. "They're getting on my last nerve, Kai. Why can't they get over the fact that Torvald and I were a horrible match?"

"Probably because they're the ones who set it up," Kai said dryly.

"Fine. A point. But shouldn't they want me to be happy?"

"You want to know something I've noticed, babe?"

She smirked. "When you're visible or when sneaking around doing invisible reconnaissance?"

"Hey!" He infused his tone with faux outrage. "I never invisibly reconnoiter. Except in extreme circumstances. Or when I can't avoid it because I'm trapped somewhere." He shuddered, the time he was stuck in a public restroom at an Interstitial club while a satyr fucked a centaur against the closed restroom door burned into his memory. Some things you could never unsee. "I'm invisible, not a voyeur."

"I know." She cupped his cheek, making her look like she was doing some kind of tai chi move in the middle of the bar. "What were you saying?"

"I was saying that I've noticed that many times when people claim they want you to be happy, they mean they want you to be *their definition* of happy. Not yours."

She sighed and dropped her hand. "I know. But I wish they could see what a good man Ole is."

He took her shoulders in a gentle grip. "I think you need to accept the fact that they may never do that, hon. And by that, I don't mean recognizing his goodness. I'm talking about them accepting him as a *man*. They might never be able to get past the fur."

Her expression lightened with a sly smile. "I don't want anyone to get past the fur except me."

Kai let go of her and clapped his hands over his ears. "La la la. Not listening."

"Oh stop." She smacked his chest. "You're not that squeamish. I've told you about my love life before."

"Yes, but not *details*."

"Ole's fur is like a full-body beard." She sniffed. "Odin should be so lucky."

He caught her hand against his heart. "Seriously, do you want me to stay? I don't mind. We can have a couple dozen more umbrella drinks—although only the nonalcoholic kind for you, little missy. I don't want you hungover on your wedding day."

"Thank you, but that won't be necessary. I have everything under control."

Under ordinary circumstance, Kai didn't doubt it. Radka might look as delicate as a flower fairy, but she had a core of pure titanium. "Are you sure? Because say the word and I'm there."

She peered up at where his eyes were. "You know I wanted you to be my main attendant, don't you? My man of honor or best man or whatever you want to call it. Right?"

He smoothed her hair. "I know."

"It means more to me than I can say that you'll be there tomorrow, even though I— Even though they—"

"Hey. It's okay." He hugged her and her arms came around him. *More tai chi moves.* "The only thing I care about is you. Making sure you and Ole get your happy ever after. In fact..." He kissed the top of her head. "Ole's best man—"

"You mean Ole's best beast?"

He pulled away so he could see her face. "You don't really think of him that way, do you?"

She gave him a disgusted glare. "Of course not. But that's what Taline and the others are calling him." She chuckled wickedly. "He scares the designer lace thongs off them."

Kai shuddered. "Ugh. Not an image I want to dwell on."

"It's probably better if you leave, anyway. Otherwise, every time you move, Baba would go on about *propuh* for ages, trying to convince me that it was a sign that the marriage is cursed, even though she knows perfectly well that you're a Klabautermann and any movement is because of you." Her expression turned sly again, and she adopted a singsong tone. "Seems like a golden opportunity for you to make a little time with the best beast."

For once, Kai was grateful for his invisibility because it meant Radka couldn't see him blush. "I, uh, don't know what you mean."

She laughed. "Come on, Kai. It's not exactly a secret. You've been crushing on Jovan since you first met him."

"That's ridiculous. He's never even *seen* me."

"Interesting." She tapped her lower lip with one finger. "I said *you* were crushing on *him*. Why should him not having seen you affect *your* feelings?"

"Because I... Because he..." Kai swallowed hard. "Oh, shit. Have I been that obvious?"

"Oh sweetie." She shook her head. "The way you two banter. The sexual tension is thick enough to cut with a rusty athame. Although we can't *see* the come-hither look you're giving him, we can feel it. And trust me, so can he." She tilted her head to peer in his general direction. "I've always wondered why you never tried to arrange an Earthside meeting with him."

"May I remind you that he's a Pure? And an ILE agent to boot?"

"So? There's bound to be a workaround if you try hard enough." She smirked at him. "You certainly seem motivated. You sext each other often enough."

"I never— We don't *sext*." Kai's face felt like it was on fire. Luckily, heat didn't activate his visibility—only incipient disaster would do that. Putting his attraction to

Jovan to the test, though? *That* was a disaster he wanted to avoid at all costs. *What if he takes one look at me and says nope, no way?* Because then Kai would lose even the potential for more and might lose Jovan as a friend too.

And despite the fact that their interactions over the two years of their acquaintance had been sparse and one-sided from the perspective of ogling—Kai got all the benefit there—they were still important. Some of the most meaningful conversations Kai had ever had were with Jovan, half drunk and bleary eyed after their poker-and-movie night get-togethers with Ole and Radka. How could he risk it?

"Kai." She ran her hands up his arms until she got to his shoulders and gripped him, her fingers digging in.

"Ow?"

"Don't be a baby. He likes you too. Ole's mentioned it to me more than once. He asks about you, oh so nonchalantly, fooling precisely no one." She smirked again. "We almost bet on it, Ole and me."

"Bet on what?" Kai said suspiciously.

"That the two of you would finally hook up this weekend."

"Oh really." Kai's growl was a fair facsimile of Jovan's. "Which one of you bet against it?"

"Neither. I said we *almost* bet on it. We didn't, because both of us wanted the *hell, yes* option. Why?" She lifted one flawless blond eyebrow. "You willing to bet against me? I'll lay you whatever odds you like that you won't be able to resist him."

Kai gazed across the room at the strong line of Jovan's spine, at the breadth of his shoulders under his white dress shirt, at the dark waves of his hair. "No bet," he croaked.

She patted his shoulder. "Good choice. Now go get him, tiger." She started to walk past him, but he grabbed her elbow.

"What if he doesn't like what he sees?"

"Kai," she said, her voice laced with annoyance, "if my wedding doesn't convince you that what's on the outside isn't as important as what's on the inside, I don't know what will do the trick. You're a wonderful guy. So is Jovan, even if he is a little prickly and might morph into a wolf when stressed. There's nothing the two of you can do until tomorrow, anyway. Ole's stuck with the bridesmaids from Hel, and I'm stuck with Baba Lenka." She shooed him with both hands. "Go! I need to know that *somebody's* getting lucky tonight, because it sure won't be Ole or me."

CHAPTER THREE

"Hey." Kai's voice at his elbow caused Jovan to slosh ginger ale over the edge of his glass. "Oh, I'm so sorry. Let me." Several bar napkins disappeared off the stack and popped back, blotting at Jovan's hand and sleeve.

"It's okay." Jovan grabbed another couple of napkins and mopped up the puddle on the bar. "Was miles away."

"Any particular location?" Kai's tone was light, teasing, and it lifted Jovan's spirits. Kai was probably the only person in the multiverse who dared tease him. To everybody else—except possibly Ole and Radka—he was the ILE's hound. Their watchdog. Their beast. Angrboða's *other* son, half-brother of Fenrir, the monster who was destined to kill Odin.

Yeah, he wasn't exactly popular on the Nine Worlds party circuit.

"Just wondering what those harpies are inflicting on poor Ole right now."

"Hey. Don't let any harpies hear you insult them like that. They have standards, you know."

Jovan snorted. "Right." Vila could be just as vicious as harpies, but they were far sneakier about it. People tended to underestimate them because they looked as angelic as…well…angels, while harpies reveled in their goth sensibilities. He pushed his glass away. Now that Ole had been borne off, there was no reason for him to stay in the bar. *Other than Kai.* "Wherever they've taken him, he'll probably need a treat once they set him free."

"Well, it won't be tonight."

Jovan frowned, staring at where Kai's voice had emanated. "What do you mean? How long does this go on?"

"They'll deliver him to his suite at the wedding venue by six tomorrow morning."

"Six? What the Hel are they going to do to him?"

Kai's chuckle didn't soothe Jovan's alarm this time. "Nothing that he doesn't consent to, don't worry. But it's a tradition to make sure that he doesn't see the bride before the ceremony."

"So instead he sees four other blond women, none of whom I'd trust farther than I could throw them?"

"Considering how petite they all are, I suspect you could heave them quite a distance."

"Don't tempt me," Jovan growled.

"You should know by now that as far as Ole's concerned, Radka's the only woman in the multiverse. Nothing sleazy will happen. There'll be supervision to make sure of it."

"Not Baba Lenka, I hope."

"No." Kai's tone held disgust. "Poor Radka's stuck with her. According to the official wedding itinerary—"

Jovan raised his eyebrows. "There's an official wedding itinerary?"

Kai punched him lightly in the biceps. "Yes, there's an official wedding itinerary. It's about twenty pages long. With footnotes. And hyperlinks. The email went out from

Enchanted Occasions last week. As the best man, you should have committed it to memory by now."

Jovan rubbed the back of his neck as heat rushed up his throat. "I, uh, may have missed that. I've been involved in a case." A case that had sent him into full Úlfheðinn transformation. He'd spent most of the last seven days as a wolf. But there was something… He squinted, trying to place the memory. "Ole mentioned there was a plan. But I figured I'd just, you know…"

"Wing it?"

"Hey." Jovan drew himself up. "I tried to get involved, but every time I made a suggestion or offered to handle a task, Ole told me it was being taken care of, either by Enchanted Occasions or Radka's family." He sighed. "Ole's pretty much handed off all the decision-making."

"Why? It's his wedding too."

"He just wants Radka to be happy. And at the moment, making her happy—"

"Means appeasing her family. Trust me. I get it. For that, Ole definitely needs treats. What did you have in mind?"

"Don't tell him I let it slip, but he has a desperate weakness for Swedish fish."

"Swedish fish? The candy?"

Jovan nodded. "And he's exhausted his stash with all the pre-wedding stress. But there's nowhere in the Interstices to get them so—"

There was a tug on his sleeve. "Come on. I know just the place."

"Where?"

"An Earthside candy shop just off the Strip. I can— Oh, blast. Pures from alternate realms can't go Earthside without risking dislocation syndrome." He sighed. "Sorry."

"Earthside?" Jovan shifted uneasily on his stool. His identity as an aitcher was hidden for a reason. For his job. *But Kai won't tell.* This might be his only chance to actually *see* Kai in the flesh. "I'm not sure—"

"Wait." Excitement infused his tone. "You've got one of those interface talismans from Enchanted Occasions, right? Radka said the whole wedding party got them for the duration of the weekend."

They'd offered Jovan one, but he'd turned it down since it wasn't necessary. *But Kai doesn't know that.* This was a perfect chance to have his *Kvæfjordkake* and eat it too, and Jovan was weak enough where Kai was concerned to give in to temptation. "Why, yes. Yes, I do."

"Then come on. Our work here is done for the moment. Unless..." Kai's voice turned uncertain. "...you'd rather not come with me?"

"No!" Jovan leaped off his stool, and judging by the resulting startled *oof*, probably nearly knocked Kai on his ass. "I mean, yes. I'd like to come with you." He glanced at the bartender who'd been polishing the same glass for the last ten minutes. "If I hang out here any longer, I'm liable to give that guy an aneurism."

"All right then." Kai chuckled. "I'd say follow me, but we know that's not really a possibility."

"You could leave a trail of breadcrumbs."

"Yes. Or I could...take your hand?"

Yes, please. Jovan extended his palm, just as large as Ole's although less furry. "Lead the way."

When Kai's fingers threaded through his, a spark *zing*ed down Jovan's spine. He let Kai pull him along, reveling in the connection, the warmth of Kai's hand in his, even though he probably looked like he was sleepwalking wide awake. *Don't care how weird it looks.* Hel, this was the Interstices. Weird was pretty much SOP.

He nodded to the bartender on the way out the door, into the perpetual twilight of the Vegas Interstices. When Jovan turned toward the public intergate, Kai tugged him in another direction.

"This way."

"I feel like a barge being maneuvered by a very bossy tugboat."

"Klabautermänner *inhabit* boats. We are not the boats themselves." Kai set a brisk pace, skirting the rather down-at-heels Twilight Carnival, the barkers' patter and the shrieks of riders on the Nine Circles of Hell roller coaster drifting out on the dry desert air. "Besides, I'm only an aitcher. I've never set foot on a boat."

"You're not *only* an aitcher," Jovan growled. "You're just as important and valuable as anybody else."

"Tell that to my father's clan. Tell that to Radka's family —or Ole's for that matter. Tell that to any Pure." Kai chuckled as he nudged Jovan to the left, toward the wide yellow brick road that spiraled out from the Interstices' heart.

That's right. An actual yellow brick road. Whichever magicians had configured this part of the Interstices had a very peculiar sense of humor. The path led to the Interstitial analog of the Vegas Strip—Interside versions of the Bellagio, the Mirage, a Cirque du Soleil tent, and more —that was as permanent as anything in the Interstices could be. If a magic user had enough skill, power, and determination, they could manifest anything in these spaces.

"I do. On a regular basis."

Kai tugged him to a stop in front of the Bellagio fountain—which, on the Interstitial side, spouted fire instead of water. "I'm sorry. I didn't mean to disparage you. I respect your work more than I can say. I always have."

With the fountain's dancing flames as a backdrop, Jovan could almost—*almost*—detect the faint outline of Kai's body. He smiled down at him. "You don't have to apologize. I know."

The vague outline nodded decisively. "Good." He tugged Jovan past the fountain. "I rented a room at the Earthside Bellagio for this weekend, so I've got access to the portal here. It's the quickest way to the candy shop."

Jovan studied his surroundings as Kai dragged him through the lobby, past the desk staffed by a couple of big-eyed sylphs. "Nice place. I've never been here before."

"Just stay out of the casino. It's run by demons, and you can't buy chips with anything as mundane as gold or diamonds." He steered Jovan toward an unobtrusive doorway behind the concierge desk.

"What do they use?"

"Let's put it this way." Kai stopped them in front of the door. "Gamblers walk in with their souls intact, but they don't always leave the same way. Or at all." He opened the door and pulled Jovan into...

"The luggage storage closet?"

Kai's laugh traveled up Jovan's arm and lodged, warm and tingly, under his heart. "They can't just leave the portal in plain sight, now, can they?"

They threaded their way past racks of suitcases and duffel bags—some of which were moving in a very disconcerting manner—to a nondescript door in a shadowy alcove at the back of the room. The keypad mounted on the wall beeped and lit up as Kai entered the code.

Jovan could have done it—as one of the few ILE agents cleared for Earthside cases, he had a master code for every threshold throughout the Interstitial network, not just here in the Vegas hub. But he wasn't willing to reveal that secret yet.

He couldn't. Literally.

By the spells on his ILE employment contract, if he revealed his own nature, he'd be rendered mute for twenty-four hours, or until ILE Internal Affairs saw fit to release him. Not only would that break his promise to Ole to support him through the wedding, but this might be his only opportunity to be with Kai, and he wasn't about to risk it.

He'd kept his mouth shut about his nature for this long. Surely he could manage another couple of days.

Kai stepped through the door, disappearing behind the chaotic swirl of the intergate, with Jovan's hand still clasped in his. "Come on, Jovan," he called, his voice distorted by the threshold's displacement field. "Swedish fish await."

He yanked on Jovan's hand, sending him stumbling forward through the dizzying disorientation that always accompanied a portal passage.

"Ooof!" He shoulder banged into something hard and angular, sending him off balance, but a warm hand on his chest steadied him.

"Careful. You don't want to cause a cascading luggage failure. This side of the hotel doesn't have a convenient mage on staff to repair the damage."

Dimly, Jovan realized Kai was speaking to him, but he couldn't have responded if his hair was on fire. Because for the first time, he was able to look Kai in the face.

And what a face.

Dark eyes behind tortoiseshell glasses. A full mouth, lifted in a wry smile and framed by scruff two shades darker than his slightly shaggy brown hair. Cheekbones. Loki's balls, the cheekbones. *I was right. He's five-ten.* Kai's shoulders were wide, his chest taut under an extremely tight Mutant Enemy T-shirt. Fit. Not overly muscled. Maybe a runner. Or maybe—

"Jovan?" Kai peered up at him from behind those adorable glasses. "Are you okay?"

"You look just like your voice," he blurted.

Kai scrunched up his face. "Geeky." He ran an elegant hand through his hair, sending a shock of it flopping over his forehead. *Argh! More adorableness!* "And like I really need a haircut."

"Nope." Jovan grinned, warming from the inside out. "Just the perfect alignment of stars." He'd lost hold of Kai when he nearly overturned the metal luggage rack, so he grabbed his hand again. Kai's lips parted, and he blinked, staring down at their joined fingers. "Do you mind?"

"No. Not a bit."

For the first time, Jovan witnessed Kai's grin, and the world shifted under his feet. Loki's balls. The tales about Klabautermänner were right.

Once you see one, you're doomed.

Kai stood in front of a row of plastic bins filled with jelly beans, sorted in color spectrum order, watching Jovan buy approximately sixteen tons of Swedish fish. Ole was a big guy, sure, and goblins of all species could rival a sarlacc pit for massive consumption—their digestive systems might as well be made of titanium. But if he ate even half of those, he'd be in a sugar coma for his entire honeymoon.

Jovan shot a glance at Kai as the cashier rang up his purchase. He'd been doing that ever since they'd crossed the threshold when Kai had become visible. *I should have worn something more attractive.* But when he'd donned his oldest skinny jeans and a worn T-shirt he'd gotten from the first FanFunCon he and Radka had attended together, he'd dressed for comfort, not style.

If he'd known Jovan would finally *see* him, he'd have made a rather more fashionable—and less ventilated—choice.

Jovan glanced at him again, and Kai couldn't tell if it was because he actually liked what he saw or if he couldn't believe his eyes. *Or maybe he just wants to make sure I don't ditch him.* Jovan couldn't have had much experience Earthside, and the Vegas Interstices wasn't an *exact* replica of its Earthside counterpart. No freaking yellow brick road on this side of the portal, for one thing.

But every time Jovan had caught Kai's gaze, he'd had a *look* in his eyes and a definite smile playing around those full lips that were so incongruous in the square jaw. As much time as Kai had spent ogling Jovan from the safety of his invisibility—which wasn't nearly as often as he'd have liked—he'd never seen this particular expression, so he wasn't sure how to interpret it.

Maybe it was good—coming down on the *I-want-to-jump-your-bones* side as opposed to the *I'm-trying-not-to-burst-out-laughing* side. Radka had sworn Jovan was interested. *But that was before he saw me. Why did I skip my salon appointment on Wednesday?*

Easy answer: a public relations crisis at the station, when Radka's replacement had predicted a monsoon in Minneapolis because she skipped a paragraph on the teleprompter and the weather map hadn't updated in time. He'd had to exercise every iota of his skill and diplomacy to A) keep his boss from firing the poor woman on the spot and B) kill the graphic before it could turn into an internet meme that would haunt them forever.

He sighed as Jovan accepted the giant shopping bag from the clerk who gazed up at him with absolute heart-eyes. *Yeah, I know the feeling.*

Jovan joined him, brandishing the bag. "All set."

"Maybe you should invest in some insulin as well, because if Ole eats all that—"

Jovan laughed, and *gah! By the North Star, I've never seen him laugh before.* Sure, he'd chuckled, chortled, guffawed a time or two during their dinners, movie nights, and poker games with Ole and Radka. But he'd never *laughed*.

"Don't worry. I ration him. But I figured I'd better stock up now, in case..." The laughter in his eyes died a little. "I suppose I won't need to maintain his stash now, will I? That'll be Radka's job."

Kai wanted to capture that laugh again, watch it transform Jovan's stern features and turn him into a dead ringer for Asgard's perpetual Sexiest Man in the Nine Worlds award winner. *Eat your heart out, Balder the*

Beautiful. You've got nothin' on Jovan Kos. He grabbed Jovan's free hand, since they'd already agreed that hand-holding was allowed.

"Hey. Just because Ole's married, it doesn't mean he won't still need his friends." Kai squeezed Jovan's fingers. "In fact, considering his in-laws, he'll probably need them more."

For a moment, Jovan looked almost vulnerable. "You really think so?"

"I know so. Plus, I have absolutely no intention of allowing Radka to ghost me in favor of her fuzzy SO." He led Jovan out of the candy store into all the manic glory of the Vegas Strip in the midst of this year's FanFunCon. "I'm not sure if I could survive without our monthly movie-slash-poker-slash-kvetch sessions. And I absolutely know that even though Radka's abandoned me for a fancy title, the best equipment money can buy, and a boss who probably won't shout at her at least six times a day, I know she'll never be able to go cold turkey on station gossip. Heck, she was one of the main sources, given that she can hear whispers on the wind." He dodged a Gandalf cosplayer, squeezing himself against Jovan's side. *Not exactly a hardship.* "In fact, I'm not sure the rest of the station crew will survive without her to..." His throat closed unexpectedly.

Jovan glanced down at him, probably waiting for Kai to finish his damn sentence, but Kai couldn't force another word out. Jovan glowered at a squad of storm troopers accompanied by a phalanx of Moira Roses and a couple of Andorians, and they scurried out of his way. He led Kai gently over to a concrete bench which cleared of a canoodling Steve and Bucky couple after one look at Jovan's glare.

He sat, pulling Kai down next to him. "You're going to miss her. Radka." It wasn't a question, and it didn't have to be.

Kai nodded. "W-we've been inseparable Earthside ever since she joined the station as meteorologist the same week I stepped from intern to executive assistant." Kai smiled wanly. "We recognized each other at once as the only supernaturals in the place. I assumed she was an aitcher at first, like me. We didn't share any supernatural credentials at first. We didn't need to. It was just such a relief not to have to hide from someone." He snorted. "Listen to me, complaining about hiding. I'm the very definition of hiding. I'm just as invisible at work as I am in the Interstices, as long as I do my job right."

Jovan made a noncommittal sound and rested their joined hands on his knee. Kai apparently hadn't learned to keep his mouth shut because the words kept tumbling out.

"She assumed I was like her—a Pure from an Earthside supernatural species, one without their own realm." Kai smiled crookedly. "She wasn't entirely wrong. Klabautermänner are Earthside natives too. It wasn't until we'd known each other a month and were getting sloshed on margaritas after a particularly brutal day at work that she told me she was a Pure. And I told her I wasn't." He looked up at Jovan. "And you know what? It didn't change a thing. We were still best friends. Still drank too many margaritas after lousy work days. Still snarked about our many annoying colleagues. I told her about getting shunned by my father's clan. She felt comfortable enough with me to tell me about her problems with Torvald and the divorce and her family's attitudes." He took a shaky breath. "I'll really, *really* miss her."

"Hey." Jovan leaned against Kai's shoulder, all muscled warmth and support. "A really smart guy once told me that just because somebody gets married, doesn't mean they won't still need their friends."

A smile tugged Kai's lips. "He did, huh?"

"Yup."

"Think he's right?"

"I know he is," Jovan said gruffly. "I've never known him to be wrong about anything."

Kai's throat thickened again. *Don't cry just because he said something sweet.* He swallowed once. Twice. Then he took his courage in both hands—and maybe all ten toes as well—and swiveled to face Jovan. *This might be my only chance.* "So, I was thinking," he said, at the same time Jovan said, "So, I was thinking—"

They stared at each other. "You first," they said simultaneously. Then, "No, you."

Jovan muttered something under his breath, rubbing the back of his neck as his scowl deepened, scaring off three Tellarites and an Uruk-hai. For some reason, Kai found it the most adorable thing ever because at the same time, Jovan was holding a pink striped bag with a metric ton of candy in his lap.

Moving slowly, Kai rested his fingertips on Jovan's enormous thigh. The muscles immediately contracted under his palm and he snatched his hand away. "Sorry."

Jovan captured it and put it back, stacking his own hand on top. "Don't be. I liked it."

Well, that's a good sign, right? Kai swallowed against his dry throat. *And the kid goes for broke.* "I think I mentioned that, um, I've got a hotel room at the Bellagio."

"You did," Jovan rumbled.

"Would you— That is, the trip back to Jotunheim isn't that long, what with the Vegas Interstices being a hub and all, and the wedding venue's in the Oslo Interstices, so I supposed it's closer than here, but—"

"Kai." Jovan lifted one eyebrow. "Are you asking me to stay with you tonight?"

"Yes?"

"In your bed?"

Kai cleared his throat. "Yes." *Drat.* His voice emerged in a very unimpressive squeak.

"There's a problem with that." Jovan gazed into Kai's eyes, and Kai couldn't have moved if the bench caught fire.

Good thing concrete isn't flammable. Mostly. "Wh-what?"

"I always sleep naked."

Kai's eyes threatened to roll back in his head. "Well, *you* may have a problem with that, but *I* certainly don't. Not a single, solitary one."

"In that case, I'd be honored to stay with you. In your bed. Naked. On two conditions."

"Name them," Kai said breathlessly.

"First, you have to be naked too."

"I can do that," Kai croaked.

"Second…" Jovan's gaze dropped, and holy crap, he actually *bit his lip.* "May I kiss you now?"

Kai nodded wildly, but Jovan stopped his bobblehead impression cold by placing one long, warm finger under

Kai's chin. And then he smiled. *Oh my stars, he has dimples!* And leaned forward slowly... slowly... slowly....

Kai huffed out an exasperated breath and closed the last millimeter. As soon as his lips touched Jovan's, every single doubt he'd ever had about his place in the world disappeared. Because this here? Now? With this man?

I'm finally home.

CHAPTER FOUR

Game. Over.

Kai's lips were soft and plush and perfect. Jovan wanted to devour him, right here in this ridiculously over-illuminated city, consume Kai's sweetness, take it into himself so he could feel all that light from the inside and brighten his dark, stunted soul.

He growled low in his throat and threaded his fingers through hair like silk, cupping the back of Kai's head gently, so gently, so his big rough hands wouldn't hurt.

How in Loki's name have I existed this long without tasting him? And how can I exist without regular repeats? Tonight? Tomorrow? Forever?

Jovan had been half in love with Kai since they'd met, but now? *Fuck.*

He forced himself to draw away, thankful that the stupid candy bag in his lap masked the state of his trousers. "I—"

"Come back!" Kai clutched Jovan's shirt. "I think we need to explore that condition a little more."

Jovan couldn't help smile down at Kai. His cheeks above his scruff were pink, his eyes a little unfocused. *So fucking gorgeous.* Jovan couldn't wait to see what happened when he took him apart. "I've heard that what happens in Vegas stays in Vegas, but I don't want one of those things to be us when we're arrested for public indecency."

Kai huffed, and *indignant* was just as adorable on him as uncertainty. *But not as adorable as blissed-out.* "Have you looked around? I'm pretty sure that Mystique cosplayer over there is actually naked except for the body paint and a couple of strategic scraps of cloth."

"Showing skin is one thing. Engaging in public sex acts would be a step too far."

"Spoilsport," Kai grumbled. "But I suppose you have a point."

Jovan stood, keeping the candy bag strategically in place, and held out a hand. "Come on and show me to your lair."

Kai took his hand, but raised his eyebrow at the candy bag. "I've heard strange men with candy frequently have sinister ulterior motives."

"The sooner we're in your room, the sooner you'll find out."

"What are you waiting for?" Kai leaped to his feet and practically towed Jovan down the sidewalk.

The crowds had thickened, the costumes getting wilder and more revealing as the night wore on. The cooler air wasn't doing much to deflate Jovan's cock, especially given Kai's obvious enthusiasm, but the third time some asshole in a Darth Vader mask knocked into Kai's shoulder, Jovan's immediate agenda changed.

Donning his patented Úlfheðinn game face—just two degrees below full berserker—he took two giant steps forward to overtake Kai. "Stay behind me."

Kai glanced up at him, brows drawn together in a scowl that wouldn't scare a wood sprite. "I live in this city. I can get around."

"I don't doubt it." He leaned down and murmured in Kai's ear. "But I've waited for two years to see your skin—*all* of your skin—and I'd rather it wasn't bruised because some asshole decided to plow into you on the street."

The proto-scowl vanished, replaced by a decided twinkle. "You want to reserve the plowing for yourself, is that it?"

Jovan barked a laugh. "Yes, that. But mostly I'm a much more efficient juggernaut. Your invisibility means you're used to dodging around people, giving the right of way to them since they can't make allowances for someone they can't see."

"They can see me now."

Trust me. I know. Jovan had already aimed his most lethal glares at a couple of blond *LOTR* elves who were eyeing Kai's ass. "But you still act like they can't." He cupped Kai's jaw and dropped a lingering kiss on his lips. "They can't miss me. So let me clear the path. I've got to be good for something."

Kai turned his head to kiss Jovan's palm and smiled up at him shyly. "You're good for *everything*."

"Hold that thought." Jovan grinned. "I'll conduct another survey in a couple of hours to see if you still agree. For now, leave this to me."

With Kai behind his shoulder, hand clasped firmly in his, Jovan faced the throng and strode forward, daring any of the Wolverines or Rens or Spocks to get in his way.

None dared. *Excellent.*

He bulldozed his way back to the Bellagio and once inside, gestured with the candy bag for Kai to lead the way. "Your turn. I don't want to terrorize the staff."

"Really?" Kai said dryly.

"Absolutely." Jovan grinned. "We might want room service later." He leaned closer and murmured, "I understand they serve a mean breakfast."

Kai's eyes widened, his Adam's apple sliding in an obvious gulp. "The elevators are over here." His sprint for the elevators was nearly as relentless as Jovan's charge down the Strip.

Unfortunately, a bellhop with a laden luggage cart and a woman in a completely unnecessary fur-collared jacket shared the elevator with them, bound for a floor above Kai's, so Jovan didn't have a chance to maul him on the way up. Once the doors slid open on Kai's floor, though, all bets were off.

Jovan crowded against Kai's back as he fumbled with his key card, nuzzling behind his ear and inhaling the ocean scent so incongruous in the desert.

"Jovan," Kai said, his voice a little strained. "I'll never get the door open if you keep doing that."

Reluctantly, Jovan stepped away and plastered himself against the wall on the opposite side of the corridor. "Sorry."

Kai glared at him—more of a glarelet, actually, from behind those sexy glasses. "I didn't mean you had to retreat to Tierra del Fuego."

"So I can—"

But the green light on the door finally lit, and Jovan hustled Kai into the room. The lights of Las Vegas spilled in through the open curtains, revealing the king-sized bed. *Yes!*

As soon as the door closed behind them, they were on each other. Odin's beard, Jovan had never wished for the extra arms of a goblin berserker, but he did now. Because two arms, two hands, weren't enough to hold Kai close, to feel him everywhere, to divest him of T-shirt and jeans.

But somehow, despite such clearly substandard equipment, Jovan managed, and Kai was standing naked in front of the wide windows, back-lit by the neon of the Strip. Jovan flicked on the bedside lamp, the better to see, and suddenly couldn't catch his breath. Kai was even more beautiful than he'd imagined.

His body wasn't overly muscled—fit, as Jovan had noted before—and his chest was smooth and hairless. A puckered scar across his hip marred the perfection of his smooth golden skin, the sight catching under Jovan's heart. *Was it an accident? Did someone hurt him on purpose?*

But thoughts of vengeance disappeared because the raised flesh seemed to point the way to Kai's cock—long, slender, cut—and any distance between them became unbearable. He stepped forward, his own shirt unbuttoned and hanging off one shoulder, to run a finger down Kai's throat and over his sternum. "So beautiful."

Kai's breath hitched when Jovan ghosted a fingertip over one copper nipple, and he grasped Jovan's wrist. "Hold on there, Agent Kos. I believe I was promised you naked."

"We'll get there. My mother's ex is the trickster, not me. I never break an oath." He edged closer, carding his fingers through Kai's hair, the lamp's gentle glow picking out unexpected gold highlights amid the brown. "But I've never seen you before. Let me look my fill? Please? Just for a little while." *Because I don't know when I'll get another chance.*

The thought that this might be the only time he and Kai could be together—his damn ILE oath was another promise he couldn't break—made Jovan's eyes prickle. Kai nodded, though, a shy smile on his lips as he peered up at Jovan through his bangs. *If this is the only time, I'll damn well make it count.*

As much as his own cock was straining against his fly, Jovan kept his hands determinedly above Kai's waist for now because there was so much he wanted to explore.

The arch of Kai's eyebrows begged for Jovan's lips, the column of his throat for Jovan's tongue, the lobes of his ears for Jovan's teeth. Everything, *everything*, was better than he'd ever imagined, Kai's skin flavored with salt, his breath warm and sweet, his gaze tender fire that Jovan swore seared straight to his heart.

And his mouth. Loki's balls, his *mouth*. Jovan could come just from kissing Kai, with nothing more than a fingertip under his jaw to improve the angle and allow his tongue to invade.

Kai broke away with a gasp and grabbed the base of his ruddy cock. "I can't— I'm going to shoot right now if you keep that up."

Guess I'm not the only one turned on by the kisses. "Me? I'm pretty sure you're participating in this too."

The glarelet was back and Kai pointed his free hand at Jovan. "You. Naked. Now. You *promised*."

"All right." Jovan shrugged his shirt off and let it fall to the floor, and, fuck, the way Kai's eyes widened, his tongue darting out to moisten his lower lip as his gaze practically devoured Jovan's chest... *My cock needs a restraining grip now.*

Forget the teasing. He needed Kai on the bed immediately. Under him, over him, beside him—it didn't matter, as long as they were touching everywhere. He shed his trousers, although his seduction technique was marred somewhat when he got one foot caught because he'd forgotten to take off his shoes first. "Fuck."

Kai chuckled, and for a moment Jovan was mesmerized. *This is what his face looks like when he makes that sound.* Then Kai took his arm and eased him down to sit on the edge of the king bed. "Let me."

Kai knelt at Jovan's feet and removed his polished loafers and socks before easing his trousers off his feet. From this angle, Jovan's cock was at perfect eye—and mouth—level, so, with one cheeky glance at Jovan, whose incendiary gaze rivaled a fire demon's, Kai teased the slit with the tip of his tongue and was rewarded with a milky bead of pre-come. *Delicious.* Jovan's moan was even more delicious.

I've heard him growl. I've heard him snarl. I've heard him shout and snark and grumble. I've never heard him moan.

And now that he had, Kai wasn't sure he'd ever get enough of the sound. But when he opened his mouth wider and leaned forward to take the head into his mouth, Jovan stopped him by cupping his jaw and easing him away.

"Not yet, baby. Come up here. Lie down with me. I want to hold you for a while first."

Kai licked his lips, almost ready to refuse because he really wanted another taste, and then he thought, *What am*

I, crazy? No way can I pass up a chance for Jovan to hold me, skin to skin, at last.

Jovan pushed the white duvet onto the blue plush bench at the foot of the bed, tossed the sheet back, and climbed aboard, his big body dwarfing the bed. He rolled onto his back and held his arms open. "Come here."

Kai's breath was doing something funny, some kind of syncopated call-and-response with his stuttering heart, because Jovan naked was...was...*gah!*

Kai knew that Jötnar were technically giants, although not all of them expressed their supernatural nature in being *actual* giants. It was more a metaphorical giantism, a larger-than-life way of approaching the world. Jötnar were *extra*. Look at Jovan's actual half siblings—Fenrir, Jormungandr, and Hel. You didn't get much more extra than a giant wolf, an ever-expanding serpent, and the literal queen of Helheim.

But Jovan was the very definition of *extra*, too. Extra gorgeous. Broad shoulders, defined abs, mouthwatering Adonis belt—not to mention the *very* extra cock jutting up from its nest of dark curls.

"Kai?" Jovan's voice held a hint of uncertainty. "Are you—"

"Wow," Kai breathed, unable to tear his gaze away from Jovan's cock. "I know you Jötnar are classed as giants, but I thought that was figurative. Not literal."

The sheet rustled as Jovan lifted onto one elbow. "Does it... frighten you? Because we don't have to—"

"No!" Kai managed to stop staring at Jovan's groin and look into his eyes instead. By the North Star, he'd never seen Jovan look uncertain before. "Nothing about you could never frighten me."

Jovan's gaze slid away from Kai's and his mouth twisted in a wry smile. "You'd be the first, then. I'm notorious, remember? Brother of monsters. The Hound of the ILE. The Beast of the Interstices. Merciless and cruel and—"

"Stop." Kai knee-walked across the bed until he was able to lay his hand on Jovan's chest. "All those things, those are just window dressing. The mask you put on to do your job, to withstand the lip-curling contempt that criminals throw at you."

Jovan sighed, but he laid his hand over Kai's. "It's more than a facade, Kai. One of the reasons I joined the ILE is because it suits me. I may not be an actual wolf like Fenrir, but I'm a Úlfheðinn. A wolf warrior and sometime berserker. It's my job to be merciless. My Jötunn nature protects me from reprisals, but those around me don't have the same defenses, the same protections. I can't afford soft targets. I wasn't even sure I should agree to be Ole's best man, because then people would know he's important to me and use him for leverage."

"I understand." He understood too well what Jovan *wasn't* saying—that he couldn't afford to let Kai get too close either, lest his enemies exploit their connection and compromise his job. *Best not to think about that now.* They had tonight. It would have to be enough. Kai stroked the silky hair on Jovan's chest. "Impressive. Not as thick as Ole's, I imagine."

Jovan snorted. "I should hope not."

"Radka likes it. She told me it was one of the first things that attracted her to him. His fur." Kai grinned. "I didn't ask how far it extended."

"He's a frost goblin. It's *everywhere*."

"Um. Good to know?" Kai's gaze drifted helplessly downward. "Extra," he murmured.

Jovan's chest vibrated under Kai's palm. He stroked Kai's arm, a feather touch at odds with his reputation and his own opinion of his nature. "It's only proportional." His gaze flicked to Kai's cock. "Same as yours."

"Not exactly reassuring in the face of...*that*, but Earthside my endowments, such as they are, at least exist."

Jovan's fingers stopped their mesmerizing trail and Kai wanted to whimper in protest, because that touch was igniting nerve endings he didn't know he possessed.

"Kai. Look at me."

Kai swallowed. "I am. Trust me."

Jovan rumbled with what Kai now recognized as a chuckle. "My eyes are up here."

Kai blinked. "Right." He focused on Jovan's face—hard to do with so much other real estate in view that he'd never had the opportunity to inspect before—and caught his breath at the *intensity* in Jovan's gaze. Fierce, but not cruel.

"You exist in the Interstices. Just because you're invisible doesn't mean you're not *there*. I know. I've felt your breath on my skin." He traced Kai's lip with a fingertip. "Your hand on my arm." He trailed his finger from Kai's bare shoulder to his wrist. "Your warmth against my shoulder." He settled both hands on Kai's waist. "So do you suppose, Kai, as a favor and only if you truly want, that I could feel your warmth against me now?"

Kai's skin tingled in the wake of Jovan's touch. "Are *you* sure?"

"So very sure." Jovan spread his legs, leaving a perfect berth for Kai, and opened his arms again.

So Kai swallowed his nerves and climbed aboard. His breath hitched when his cock nestled against Jovan's like it had found its home port. His hips were narrower than Jovan's. He was narrower than Jovan everywhere, but that only made it more perfect. *We fit.*

The roughness of Jovan's chest hair against his own hairless one, a tantalizing brush against his nipples, made Kai moan, and Jovan caught the sound in a kiss. *Talk about extra.* No more gentleness, but it wasn't rough. Passionate. As if Jovan had been bottling up an inner fire and was free at last to let it rage.

Kai's hips flexed helplessly, his cock sliding against Jovan's, although maddeningly without much friction. *So what?* Just the feel of Jovan's skin against his, smooth-rough with hair, of Jovan's arms around him, tight but not restrictive, Jovan's mouth on his as if Kai's taste was more intoxicating than honeyed wine.

It was enough. More than enough. Because Kai had been dreaming about this impossibility for two years, and now it was real. And even if this could never happen again, one night was orders of magnitude better than none.

Jovan tore his mouth from Kai's. "Freya, Kai. I never..." His back arched, his teeth clenched in a grimace that looked more like pain than pleasure, his own hips bucking under Kai, and when wet warmth spread between them, the scent of Jovan's spend sent Kai over the edge too and he buried his head in Jovan's neck, gasping through his release.

Kai's breath gradually returned to normal—or at least as normal as it ever got when he was in Jovan's vicinity—and he started to roll off, but Jovan's arms tightened around his ribs.

"Stay."

"If I stay too long, we'll be glued together and have to make a very awkward 9-1-1 call. They may have to use the Jaws of Life to separate us."

"It's jizz, Kai, not superglue."

Kai pushed himself up so he could see Jovan's face, because the laughter buried in his voice must mean—yep, he was grinning. "Are you sure? I mean, the first Jötunn created the Nine Worlds from their body—"

Jovan scowled, but it was...lighter than his default glower, tempered as it was by that grin or maybe post-orgasmic dopamine. "That wasn't exactly their choice. And they didn't exactly jack off during the creation bloodbath."

"I know. Sorry. Didn't mean to be disrespectful."

"Nah. It's okay." He heaved a sigh, his ribcage expanding and lifting Kai a good six inches. "That was a long time ago."

Kai nestled his head in the angle of Jovan's shoulder. "But you've got all that yummy chest hair. Some of it might get ripped out if we wait too long, and judging by Radka's grousing before her Brazilian appointments, I don't think you want that."

Jovan winced. "You may be right." His arms tightened around Kai's ribs and he rolled them to the side. "Wait here and I'll get something to clean us up." He kissed Kai's eyebrow, his cheek, his lips. "Because we've got all night and there's lots more of you I want to explore."

"That's right." Kai settled back, hands laced behind his head as he watched Jovan cross to the bathroom, his ass flexing in a *most* distracting fashion. "I was promised you naked all night, and I intend to collect."

Kai's bone-melted afterglow was invaded by a niggle of regret. *Would* one night be better than none? Or would he have been better off not knowing what he was missing?

But Jovan lived in Jotunheim and worked in the Interstices. Kai lived and worked Earthside. They could never be together long term. Although maybe, if Kai paid a lot of money or sold his soul to the demon realm, he could acquire another interface talisman—or maybe a couple dozen—from the Enchanted Occasions magicians and arrange another Earthside visit for Jovan.

Assuming he wants one.

Jovan padded back to the bed, very light on his feet for such a big guy, and gently mopped up Kai's belly. "You know the upside of you being invisible at the wedding tomorrow?"

Kai's heart sank. "There's an upside?"

"Absolutely." He set the cloth on the glass-topped bedside table, climbed onto the bed and took Kai into his arms and the open-mouthed kiss on Kai's throat was... *gah!*

That would leave a mark for sure. Kai clutched at Jovan's shoulders, his hips bucking uncontrollably.

"The upside," Jovan mumbled against Kai's skin before drawing back to grin down at him, "is that I can leave as many hickeys on you as I want and nobody will ever know."

CHAPTER FIVE

The ping of Jovan's cell phone woke him from a sound sleep when it was still dark outside the hotel window—or as dark as it ever got in Earthside Vegas. He peered blearily at the digital clock next to the bed. 6:01. Kai had mentioned that Ole would be returned from his "kidnapping" by six, so chances were that the message was from him.

He let his head fall back. With Kai nestled against him, his head pillowed on Jovan's chest, Jovan didn't want to move. But it was Ole's wedding day, and Jovan had responsibilities.

He eased out from under Kai, trying not to wake him, but Kai peered up at him, blinking sleepily. Without his glasses, his dark eyes were luminous even in the dimness.

Kai pushed his hair off his forehead. "Is something wrong?"

"I doubt if it's anything other than Ole's nerves. If it were an emergency, he'd call instead of text." Jovan kissed Kai's forehead. "But one way or another, duty calls."

Reluctantly, he sat up, separating himself from Kai's warmth and delicious scents—his usual fresh ocean fragrance now mixed with the musk of their lovemaking.

Kai traced a pattern on Jovan's back that he recognized all too well: the sigil of his ILE tattoo. "I've heard about these."

Jovan glanced over his shoulder. The sight of Kai rumpled and sleepy, with Jovan's love bites dotting his smooth, honey-colored flesh, sent a pulse of *want* through his middle to land smack on his dick. *No time.* Besides, he knew by now that once more would never be enough. Not with Kai. Not with the only man who'd ever touched him without fear or contempt or ulterior motives.

"What have you heard?"

"That they're your passport to any realm except Earthside." Kai's eyes widened, and he bolted upright. "Shit, the talisman. The one from Enchanted Occasions. Aren't you supposed to keep it on your person at all times Earthside or risk..." He flapped both hands. "... something that nobody ever specifies? Translocation syndrome or...I don't know...death and untold destruction?"

Jovan chuckled, a sound that came much more easily to him in Kai's presence. "I feel fine. Do I look sick?" Kai shook his head. "Dead?"

Kai scowled as he fumbled his glasses off the bedside table. "Don't joke. There wouldn't be rules if there weren't at least a kernel of truth in the rumors."

He wasn't wrong, but Jovan couldn't risk telling him why he didn't need the talisman. *Because I'm just as much an aitcher as you.* "Maybe I'm in close enough proximity to prevent the worst." He stood up and wrestled his cell phone out of his crumpled trousers. He peered at the message, frowning as Kai climbed out of bed to join him, looping an arm around Jovan's waist.

"Is it an emergency after all?"

"I can't tell. He's already at the venue in the Oslo Interstices, but for some reason he wants me to meet him in a broom cupboard."

"Broom cupboard? Are you sure?" Jovan held up his phone so Kai could see the screen. "Well, that's a broom emoji. But I don't know what that word is."

"Ole's fingers are so big he has trouble texting sometimes. But I'd best go see what's up."

Kai smirked. "Yes, since you are the *best* man."

Jovan glanced down at himself. He had dried jizz in his chest hair and along his hip. "I should take a quick shower. I don't know if they've got one at the venue." He grinned at Kai. "I'd ask you to join me, but then it wouldn't be quick."

Kai's answering smile was crooked, sending a pang through Jovan's heart. *He knows it's almost over.* "Go ahead. I'll see if I can get your clothes in a more or less reputable state." He picked up Jovan's shirt, but even though he gave it a couple of sharp shakes, the wrinkles were obvious. "It wouldn't do your reputation any good to do a walk of shame to Ole's wedding."

"Oh, I don't know." He titled Kai's chin up for a kiss. "Aren't walks of shame traditional for weddings?"

"Maybe, but how does that fit with your big, tough, wolf warrior slash implacable ILE agent image?"

"You think anybody'll have the balls to comment on it?"

Kai grinned. "Good point."

While Jovan scrubbed his way through the Nine Worlds' quickest shower, he pondered the question of how he could fit Kai into his life without compromising his ILE oath or putting Kai in danger. Aitchers, probably because of the bias they faced in their supernatural parent's home realm, often embraced a life of crime Earthside, where they could capitalize on paranormal abilities that humans would never suspect. Living here, Kai would be a target if they suspected he could be used as leverage.

Jovan sighed as he dried off. *Not a problem I can solve today.* Today was for Ole and Radka. But he was definitely putting it on the front burner.

When he emerged from the bathroom amid a cloud of steam with a towel around his waist, Kai was dressed in his jeans and T-shirt again and was just placing Jovan's neatly pressed shirt on a hanger.

"I've got them into a reasonable state, I think, so if..." His voice died as he gazed at Jovan. "Wow. It's like you just stepped out of the fires of creation. The perfect man."

"Hardly perfect." Jovan wore the marks of his profession on his skin: the parallel scars of a chupacabra's claws across his ribs, the chimera's bite mark on his biceps, the puckered burn from a dragon's breath on his calf. But more than that, his Úlfheðinn nature disqualified him for anything approaching perfection, as he was reminded every day. "Just ask anyone."

Kai's eyes narrowed as he stalked toward him, the hanger hooked over one finger. But when Jovan reached for the shirt, Kai snatched it behind his back. "I don't need to ask anyone. I have the evidence right here in front of me." He bent and pressed a kiss to the claw scar. "Evidence of a strong, brave, principled man who cares more about what's right than about his own comfort or safety." Then he punched Jovan in the biceps. Hard.

"Ow!" Jovan rubbed his arm. "What was that for?"

"For not taking better care of yourself. You may play fast and loose with your own well-being, Jovan, but some people take exception to that. Ole does. Radka does." He peered up at Jovan, his eyes shining behind his glasses. "I do. You *matter*. To us."

A smile tugged at Jovan's lips. "Well, in that case, I'll try to do better."

Kai nodded decisively. "Good. Now we'd better get you ready. Best man duties await." He slipped the shirt off the hanger and held it up so Jovan could slide his arms into it. "I'll walk you down to the portal."

Jovan buttoned his shirt as Kai retrieved his perfectly pressed trousers. "I can wait if you need to shower. We can go together."

"I don't have to show up until closer to the ceremony. I couldn't get near Radka anyway, not with Taline, the maid of honor from Helheim, channeling Fafnir and guarding her as if she were the Nibelungen's lost hoard." He shrugged. "If I wander around on my own, I'd only get in everybody's way and risk another *propuh* crisis." He grinned wryly. "I doubt Radka's wedding gown would be improved by one of Baba Lenka's signature mud-colored mufflers."

"I doubt anything would be." Jovan eyed his tangled briefs. *Do I bother?* Nah. He had another set at the wedding venue along with his tux, so he tossed this pair into the trash.

Kai waggled his eyebrows. "Commando. How adventuresome."

Jovan pulled on his trousers and tucked in his shirttails. "Since you won't be with me, I think I'll probably be safe."

"Hey! You make it sound like I sneak up on unsuspecting Úlfheðinn and attack them with surprise wedgies."

"No." He pulled Kai in for a kiss. "But without your voice in my ear, it'll be a lot easier to keep my dick under control, even without the extra layer."

The flush on Kai's cheeks was adorable, and Jovan's belly hollowed. *Is this the last time I'll see his face?*

"Come on," Kai said, "before I throw you down on the bed and mess you up again."

"You think you could throw me down?"

Kai lifted his chin and winked. "Well, someone would go down. One way or another."

Jovan barked a laugh and tucked his cell into his pocket. He grabbed the candy bag and held out his other hand for Kai. "Let's go then, before I take you up on that."

Although nobody was in the elevator with them, they only stood next to one another, fingers laced, unspeaking, all the way to the lobby. Kai led them past the concierge desk and into the luggage storage closet, everybody ignoring him as though he were as invisible here as he was in the Interstices, and as if he'd extended that invisibility to Jovan.

Before Jovan could think about that too much, they arrived at the portal. Kai turned to him and took a deep breath. "This has been—"

"I want to say—" Jovan said at the same moment.

"You first," they both said at once.

Jovan laughed and shook his head, letting go of Kai's hand to cup his cheek. "I know we can't expect a repeat of last night. You've got your life. I've got mine. But I want you to know that—"

Kai stopped his words with a finger across Jovan's lips. "I know. No promises. But we'll still be friends. We've got those Interstitial movie and poker nights to look forward to, right?"

"Yeah." Jovan swallowed thickly. "Of course we do." He kissed Kai then, and if it tasted of desperate longing, Jovan wasn't about to apologize for it. "I'll see you at the wedding."

"No." Kai's smile was crooked. "You won't."

Kai trudged back through the lobby and poked the elevator call button with extreme prejudice. "Why did I think this was a good idea?" he muttered. Nobody paid any attention to him, of course. He could probably splash naked in the fountain and nobody would notice.

Okay, maybe they'd notice *that*, but until Jovan, nobody had ever really *seen* him. Even Radka didn't push too far past their shared work experience and common supernatural roots because she had so many other friends and interests. Plus, she had Ole.

But Jovan, like Kai, didn't really have anybody else, and that focus, that attentiveness to Kai's *person* was... extraordinary. *I think he sees me even when I'm invisible.*

He stomped into the elevator and scowled at his reflection all the way to his floor. It wasn't nearly as impressive as Jovan's ILE game face. *I'm gonna have to practice.* On the other hand, he had a feeling he wouldn't need to practice—a scowl was about to become his default expression too.

Because I want more. I want him again. I want him every night. He sighed as the alarm pinged for his floor. Mr. Spock was wrong in that old *TOS* episode, when he informs his ex that *having* isn't as pleasant as *wanting.* Having was orders of magnitude better than wanting.

But Kai would have to settle for *wanting* from now until Ragnarok, because *having* was off the table.

He sighed as he keyed open his room, missing Jovan's heat at his back from the last time. "Stop. Just stop," he ordered himself. Not that it would do much good. When had he ever listened to his own good advice? He could solve any snafu at the station, keep the newsroom running like a well-oiled clockwork ninja, keep his temperamental boss purring like a kitten, but he couldn't wrangle his own damned heart.

He stared around the room, at the ironing board still standing next to the window, at the bed with its rumpled sheets and bunched duvet. He had hours before he needed to be at the wedding, and the trip to the Oslo Interstices would only take minutes since Vegas was an Interstitial hub and he didn't have to take multiple hops.

He could crawl back in bed and nest there, tormenting himself with the mingled scents of Jovan and sex. He could order room service and try to soothe himself with raspberry crepes and bacon. *Extra* bacon. He could go down to the casino and lose money he couldn't afford at blackjack—at least once the dealer noticed he was sitting at the table.

He snorted. *Stop being such a pathetic weenie.* His best friend was getting married today, and even though Kai couldn't be as big a part of the celebration as both of them would have preferred, he owed it to Radka and Ole to be as gods-bedamned *celebratory* as they deserved.

So he ripped off his T-shirt, kicked off his jeans and stalked into the bathroom. It had a glass-doored shower *and* an enormous bathtub. The shower doors were still beaded with the aftermath of Jovan's shower. Kai followed the path of one drop with a finger as it trickled down the inside of the glass. *First, I'll wallow in the tub for an hour or so. And then I'll take a shower. Stand where he stood. Use the same shampoo and body wash.*

Because nothing cured a broken heart like reminding it repeatedly what it had lost.

An hour and a half later, he emerged from the bathroom to the ringing of his cell phone as it vibrated across the desk. He glanced at the screen and dropped his towel, lunging the last couple of steps when he saw Jovan's name on caller ID.

"Hello?"

"Kai. Thank goodness. Where have you been?" Jovan's voice, usually a sexy rumble, was edged with…was that panic?

"I was in the bathtub. And the shower."

"The bathtub *and* the— Never mind. We've got a…a *situation* here, and you're the only one who can help. Can you get to the venue right away?"

"Sure." Kai scrabbled in the dresser drawer for a clean pair of boxer briefs. "What kind of situation are we talking about?" Silence. "Jovan? Are you still there?" The cellular connection between Earthside and the Interstices was sketchy at best.

"Yeah. I'm here. But I think it's something you really have to"—Jovan's voice was strangled—"see."

Gooseflesh rose on Kai's exposed skin. "Okay. I'll be there as soon as I can."

"Look for me outside the broom cupboard. Second floor."

"Jovan—" But the connection was gone.

Kai ripped open the closet. His wedding suit was still in its garment bag. Should he wear it? *Why?* It's not like anybody would see it—he wasn't entirely sure why he'd bought a new suit for the event, anyway. But he'd wanted to honor Radka and Ole, even if the only person who knew about the honor was himself.

But a suit might not be, er, suitable for the situation at hand. *I can always change later.* So he pulled on a soft dark blue T-shirt and his most comfortable jeans. He hesitated with his hand on his gray blazer. If the wedding were in the Vegas Interstices, he wouldn't need it. But the Oslo Interstices on the first of February? *Better safe than sorry.* He shrugged into the blazer, slipped his feet into his loafers, tucked his phone in his pocket, then shouldered his garment bag and headed out.

Once through the portal into the Vegas Interstices, he regretted donning the blazer, because by the time he'd followed the yellow brick road—*seriously?*—he was already overheated. Not very many people were around, so he didn't have to play his usual game of dodge-'em-'cause-they-can't-dodge-you. He strode past the Twilight Carnival, a few half-hearted squeals from somebody riding the rickety roller coaster following him into the undeveloped spaces in front of the portal array.

While Vegas was an Interstitial hub with portals to every other Interstices on the planet—and some beyond, if rumor was correct—you still had to pick the right one or you could end up in very uncomfortable circumstances. Ole's Uncle Snorre had miscalculated and emerged in the middle of a Muspelheim lava lake instead of his home ice realm of Niflheim. That's how he ended up a draugr, the Norse version of a zombie.

Kai found the right portal—and triple-checked his choice, because zombie conversion was *not* on his agenda for the day—and stepped through.

Okay, now *I'm glad of the blazer.* In fact, he wished for a full snowsuit, because the Oslo interstices was a winter wonderland, ice sculptures depicting dragons and hippogriffs and gryphons lining a winding path that led toward a vast, glittering castle—the wedding venue. *At least I* hope *they're just sculptures.* Because as he hurried down the path, the ice creaked and each statue's eyes seemed to follow him.

He was shivering when he stepped through the castle doors, breathing a sigh of relief when he realized that although the place glittered like ice, it was actually quite warm inside. Damn, the magicians on the Enchanted Occasions staff must be really good if they could transform an abandoned ski lodge on the verge of collapse into *this* in less than two weeks.

As Kai made his way toward a vast staircase that split midway to lead to left and right balconies overlooking the cavernous entry, he had to dodge two brownies laden with stacks of snowy linens, a skittish bwci toting a cauldron nearly as large as he was, and a woman with the slightly green skin and webbed fingers that marked her as an undine aitcher. Since all of them were wearing navy trousers, white shirts, and gray blazers with a stylized *EO* on the breast pocket, he made the leap that these were Enchanted Occasions employees.

Good thing I'm invisible. In his current outfit, he could almost be mistaken for one of them.

He ran up the stairs, his less than quiet footsteps earning a perplexed frown from a blond man in an EO blazer who was racing down the other side of the stairs. But since the man didn't stop his headlong rush, Kai didn't bother to slow his own roll, footsteps be damned.

At the landing, he paused. Left or right? Jovan had only said the second floor, not which wing of the second floor. *Which side does the groom's family traditionally sit on?* Kai couldn't remember. He hadn't been to that many weddings, and since he wasn't part of this one, he hadn't read up on all the protocols.

But then he caught sight of Jovan peeking out of a corridor on the right-hand side. His scowl somehow managed to convey more worry than intimidation, even though it looked almost the same as his usual expression. *Maybe I've just figured out how to interpret them better. Go me.*

He raced up the last set of stairs, and while he was still two arms'-lengths away, Jovan straightened up, squinting right at Kai's position.

"Kai?"

Kai's heart gave a joyous sideways bump. *He sees me.* "Yeah, I'm here."

"I thought so. I saw those banners flutter when you passed by."

Okay, so maybe he doesn't see me. "What's going on?"

Jovan crept toward the bannister and craned his neck to peer down into the entryway where EO staff still scurried about, while staying mostly out of sight. Seemingly satisfied, he jerked his chin toward the corridor. "Come with me." He strode off, his longer legs making it necessary for Kai to trot to keep up. He stopped in front of a nondescript wooden door and grasped the handle. His shoulders rose and fell with a huge breath, and he looked to his left. Unfortunately, Kai was on his right.

"I'm over here."

Jovan didn't turn to face him. Instead, he leaned his forehead on the door and took another deep breath. "Whatever you do, don't scream."

Kai blinked. "Uh…"

Then Jovan cracked the door open. The room beyond was dark and Jovan slipped inside like a shadow, then motioned for Kai to follow. "Shut the door behind you as soon as you're inside. Ole, I brought Kai."

Kai edged inside and eased the door closed. "I'm in."

"Okay." Jovan huffed another breath. "Remember. Don't scream." He flipped on the light.

Kai sucked in a breath and fumbled with his garment bag, making heavy business of hanging it on the edge of a shelf to give him time to bury his horrified reaction. Because Ole Olesson was cowering in the corner amid the brooms and pails and mops, wrapped in a white terrycloth robe from a well-known Vegas Interstitial spa.

At least, Kai *assumed* it was Ole. He was the right height —or would be if he wasn't hunched over like that—and he had Ole's big brown eyes. But all of Ole's beautiful black-tipped silver fur was gone. Pink skin, angry, welted, and inflamed, covered his face, neck, hands, and calves— all the skin that wasn't hidden by his robe.

"Hi, Kai." Ole bit his lip. "I, um, got waxed."

CHAPTER SIX

"Oh, Ole."

Kai's sympathetic tone was a damn sight different from Jovan's reaction when he'd found Ole hiding out in here. He'd had to beat down his Úlfheðinn instinct to seek out the bridesmaids who'd perpetrated this outrage and make them fucking pay. Hazing the groom was supposed to be the *groomsmen's* job, led by the best man, which is why there hadn't been any at Ole's bachelor party.

Jovan forbade it, and the other groomsmen were intimidated enough by the threat of a potential berserker reprisal that they'd agreed.

He hadn't reckoned with the bridesmaids.

Jovan turned toward Kai, and for a moment, he could have sworn he saw a glint of Kai's glasses and a hint of brown hair. *Probably my overactive wish-list.* "I thought you said that kidnapping bullshit wasn't supposed to be dangerous."

Kai's sigh ruffled Jovan's hair. "I said they couldn't do anything he didn't *consent* to." Kai's footsteps left Jovan's side and approached Ole. "Did you agree to this, Ole?" Ole nodded. "Why?"

Ole scratched at a cluster of reddened blemishes on his neck and winced. "They said Radka would like it."

"But Ole," Kai said gently, "Radka loves your fur."

"She *says* so. But she's just being nice."

"Radka is my best friend, so I say this from a place of love. She is *never* shy about expressing her opinions, and nobody has *ever* accused her of sparing someone's feelings just to be *nice*. I mean, she *is* nice. She goes out of her way for people she loves. But she's not a doormat by any means. And she doesn't lie." Kai chuckled, and something stirred below Jovan's belt because now he knew what Kai's face looked like when he made that sound. "That's something that our station administrators discovered when they wanted her to soft-pedal a report about global warming."

Ole's face scrunched up, and without the fur he just looked so...vulnerable, like a newly hatched sparrow. "Taline told me that Radka's ex-husband had beautiful skin, and that Radka said it was his best feature."

"I think her words were that it was his only good feature," Kai said dryly. "The man was a total douche."

"I've gotta ask." Jovan edged closer to Ole, careful not to make any sudden lunges for fear he'd knock Kai into a shelf full of bleach and steel wool. "Did you get waxed *all over*?" When Ole nodded again, Jovan winced and a quiet *oof* emanated from the air to his left.

"What am I going to do, Jovan?" Ole looked at him with big, sad eyes. "I can't let anyone see me like this. I can't let Radka see me like this. And the wedding is in a few hours."

"You—" Jovan picked up an empty bucket and upended it. "—are going to sit here for the moment. Kai and I will fix this."

"We will?" Kai's tone said *what the fuck* more clearly than if he'd said the words out loud. "I mean, we will. Absolutely."

He reached out to squeeze Ole's shoulder and thought better of it, because *yowtch*. "We'll be back as soon as we can with a plan. Will you be okay for a bit?"

Ole nodded miserably as he sank onto the bucket, which groaned in a rather alarming manner. Even industrial-grade plastic strained to hold up under a guy Ole's size. Although he did look much smaller without the fur.

"Kai, you're with me," Jovan said and dodged brooms and buckets to get to the door. He poked his head out, but the corridor was empty. *Yeah, because this is the groom's wing and all the other worthless groomsmen are sleeping off their hangovers.* They probably wouldn't show up until an hour before the wedding. At any other time, Jovan would have been annoyed and dragged them out of bed to do their duty. But at this particular moment, he was glad they were a bunch of entitled slackers.

With one last glance at poor Ole, sitting forlornly on his impromptu stool, hands between his knees, like a *Before* photo in an ad for Pandora pox remedies, Jovan slipped out of the closet. He stood with his back against the wall until the slight shift in the air and the door closing apparently on its own signaled that Kai had joined him.

"I'm going to kill them." Anger vibrated in Kai's voice, and with a jolt, Jovan realized he'd never heard Kai angry before. He was always such a sunny guy. "Not today. Not tomorrow. Maybe not even next week, because at the moment Ole and Radka are the only ones who matter. But someday, when they least expect it." He laughed, low and a little evil, and it went right to Jovan's dick. "They'll never see me coming."

"While I agree with the sentiment, I also agree that we have to table it for later." Jovan ran a hand through his hair. "How the Hel do we fix this?"

From the *pop* in the air, Kai had just snapped his fingers. "The event planners. They've got magicians on staff. Maybe they've got a solution. Or at least can arrange an illusion to get Ole through the ceremony."

Why didn't I think of that? "You're right. Who's in charge?"

"If you'd checked your itinerary..." Kai said, his tone amused.

"Kai." The telltale heat of a wolf rage simmered just under Jovan's skin, but suddenly a warmth and pressure on his chest—*Kai's hand*—dialed it back.

"Shhh. Sorry. I'm not sure, but we can ask. They're everywhere downstairs and pretty easy to spot since they're all wearing the same outfit. I'll— Crap." Kai muttered something else under his breath. "There's no way I'll be able to catch their attention."

"Leave that to me." Jovan squared his shoulders. "But if you're up for it, I've got another assignment for you."

"'Assignment?'" Although Kai's voice was still laced with anger, that earlier amusement bled back in. "First you bark *you're with me* and now you're giving me an assignment?" Unseen arms wrapped around Jovan's waist and Kai was *there*, unseen but not unfelt, pressed up against him from chest to...*urgh*...groin. "Tell me, Agent Kos. Does that mean I'm on your team?"

"S-sorry." Jovan swallowed, his mouth dry, unnerved in a way he never was when on a job. *But this isn't a job. It's more. It's our friends' happiness.* "I should have asked instead of barking at you."

Kai chuckled, and the vibrations sent another spark of arousal straight to Jovan's balls. "It's okay. I kind of liked it. Makes me feel…" Was that Kai's tongue on his throat? "…dangerous. Important."

"You are important." And Loki's balls, was he ever dangerous.

Kai let go and stepped away. *Damn it.* "Thank you. What do you want me to do?"

With great restraint, Jovan didn't adjust himself in his pants. "See if you can get to Radka. Tell her that…that…"

"That her maid of honor is an evil lying weasel?"

"Maybe not that. Not yet, anyway. But let her know that there's a little problem. We're dealing with it, but there might be…adjustments to today's agenda."

"Got it." Kai's kiss was unfortunately brief, but no less appreciated for all that. *Unfair. He can aim, but I can't.* "Good luck."

Rapid footsteps faded down the hall before Jovan could make a grab and feel Kai against him once more. *For luck.*

"Yeah, yeah," Jovan muttered to himself as he strode toward the staircase. "Tell it to the Valkyries."

He pounded down the stairs toward a cluster of people in matching navy trousers and gray blazers. One of them, a woman, was clearly half undine, judging by her greenish skin tone. One of the men was tall and olive-skinned, with curly black hair and the profile of a Greek statue. The other man, a smaller, compact blond with almost elfin features, was consulting a tablet. Jovan strode over to them, and the way the taller man's eyebrows rose must mean that Jovan was in full ILE agent mode. *Beast mode,* his colleagues at the agency called it, one step away from wolf berserker. *If the seven-league boot fits...*

On the other hand, he wanted help from these people, so maybe he needed to tone it down a bit. "You're with the event planning company?" He didn't think he growled. Much.

The taller man held out his hand for Jovan to shake. "Yes. I'm Mikos Iordanou, the owner. These are my colleagues, Brooke Tidewater"—Jovan shook the undine's hand—"and Anders Skuldsson."

Jovan blinked as he shook the blond man's hand. "Skuldsson? As in *the* Skuld?"

Anders sighed. "Yes. I'm half norn."

"But I thought all norns were female. And Skuld is one of the—"

"The big three. Norn with a capital N. But I assure you, I *never* interfere in the fate of any person."

Anders's emphasis on *person* was interesting, but Jovan dismissed his curiosity for the moment. "I'm Jovan Kos."

Brooke perked up. "Oh! The best man."

"Yes. And we've got a bit of a...situation."

Mikos's noble brow creased in the most elegant frown Jovan had ever seen. "A situation? What kind of situation?"

"Well..." Jovan carded his fingers through his hair. "It might be better to show you." He shot Brooke an apologetic glance. "Just the men, if you don't mind."

Brooke grinned, the silver hoop in her lower lip glinting in the light from the massed candles in the giant chandelier overhead. "I'm more than happy to leave this to Mikos and Andy. I've got my own problems."

Jovan scowled, causing all three of the others to blink. *Tone it down.* "What kind of problems?"

"Don't worry," she said brightly. "Nothing we can't handle." She flitted away.

Mikos gestured for Jovan to precede him. "Please. Lead the way, and be assured that whatever the issue, we'll take care of it. Enchanted Occasions is committed to our clients' complete satisfaction. It's our absolute guarantee."

Jovan lifted an eyebrow. "Guarantee, huh? Then come on. Because I've got one for your books."

Kai crept along the corridor, the plush carpet in the bride's wing muffling his footfalls. *Wonder why the bride's side gets carpet and the groom's side doesn't?* For that matter, even though Kai had told Ole that Radka never backed down from her convictions, she'd certainly caved on a lot of the details for the wedding.

Wonder if that's why she hasn't said much about the arrangements to me. Normally Radka told him everything, and she'd been quite forthcoming about everything *after* the wedding—a little too much so about the preparations for their honeymoon in an igloo in Norway where they could watch the Aurora Borealis while they— *Nope. Not thinking about that.* Especially not with Ole in his current furless state.

But other than apologizing to Kai for not making him part of the bridal party, and declaring that she was leaving most of the arrangements to Enchanted Occasions, it seemed like she'd deferred to her family and *other* friends —the Pures, like that poisonous Taline—for everything about a day that should be *her* dream. Hers and Ole's.

Could she still be atoning for ending her first marriage? Because if so, that was utter and complete shit. Kai's growl rivaled Jovan's best and earned a wide-eyed squeak from a passing brownie.

We made a vow, Jovan and I, and we'll keep it. One way or another, Radka and Ole would get their happy ever after, even if it meant Kai had to sneak around the bride's wing like a total creeper.

He sighed, hands on his hips, as he surveyed the corridor. All the doors—and there were a shit-ton of them—were closed tight. Not only didn't he know which one hid Radka, but he couldn't very well open each one to check. Either Baba Lenka would blame *propuh* and load Radka and everybody else within reach under acres of bad knitting, or one of the bridesmaids—who all knew Kai's nature—would figure out it was him and accuse him of being a perv.

Frankly, he wasn't sure which would be worse.

But as he was dithering in the middle of the hall, the undine in the EO blazer came dashing toward him. For a moment, he thought she might actually be able to see him and was about to speak, but when she glanced at the tablet in her hand without slowing, he leaped out of the way before she could mow him down.

She approached the second door from the end of the hallway and knocked softly. "Radka? It's Brooke."

The door opened to reveal Taline—Kai had to suppress another growl—snowdrops adorning her elaborate blond updo. "Come in," she said, her voice as cold as a frost giant's balls. "We were just discussing the musician issue."

Musician issue?

Taline held the door wider to admit Brooke and started to close it. *Shit!* Kai darted forward and slid inside, keeping his eyes averted in case any of the women were in dishabille.

"I've spoken to Smith, our tech demon," Brooke said in a businesslike fashion. "He's confident he can pipe in appropriate music that will perfectly simulate the string quartet."

"I'm afraid that isn't acceptable," Taline replied in a voice that made Kai shiver.

He dared a peek. No naked women, thank goodness. But no Radka either. Just Taline and the other three bridesmaids, whom he still couldn't tell apart, although at least now they were wearing different colored dresses: palest ice pink, blue, and green. Taline was in lavender. The fabric shimmered in the light. Collectively, they looked like sun-kissed icicles, and Taline's voice certainly fit the theme—minus the sun.

"When we met with Radka and Ole," Brooke began, to a derisive snort from Ice Pink Bridesmaid, "they both agreed to the music contingency plan."

Taline waved her hand dismissively. "That's irrelevant."

"It's in the contract, so it isn't irrelevant."

Taline fixed Brooke with a steely glare. "I believe Enchanted Occasions guarantees client satisfaction."

"Yes. We do. But—"

"Canned music will definitely not satisfy us."

Brooke's eyes narrowed, although she didn't drop her smile. "With all due respect, you're not the client. If I could speak to Radka—"

"She's having her massage now, so no, you can't. However," Taline smiled condescendingly, "since

Enchanted Occasions clearly isn't capable of meeting the most basic requirements, *I've* arranged for another musician. A famous violinist, one with *far* greater fame than the quartet who can't bother to show up."

"They're trapped by a mining protest in Svartalfheim. Heimdall shut down all the intergates."

Taline sniffed. "Whatever." She strolled over to the window and looked down. From where Brooke stood, she wouldn't be able to see Taline's face, but Kai could. Malicious satisfaction and avid anticipation. *She's up to something else. Something other than ripping Ole's fur out by the roots.* But what? "As with any great artist, there are, of course, conditions. You will need to procure a live goat."

"A goat." Brooke's tone held barely contained disbelief.

"Yes. And a marble bath, at least a meter in depth, filled with water fresh from Ofotfjord."

"The wedding is in three hours—"

Taline fixed Brooke with a triumphant glare. "Are you saying you're incapable of handling a simple request?"

Brooke straightened her shoulders. "Of course not." She made a note on her tablet. "If you'll excuse me, I'll go set things in motion."

"You do that," Taline said, low and threatening. The three ice maidens tittered and shared conspiratorial glances as Brooke headed for the door. As much as Kai wanted to stay and hear what else they had up their nonexistent sleeves, he couldn't risk being trapped in here with them, so he scuttled over to the door and whisked out ahead of Brooke when she paused to turn back to Taline.

"Please let Radka know that I stopped by. I'll check in with her after her spa treatments."

Taline didn't answer. She simply shut the door in Brooke's face.

For a moment, Brooke didn't move. She stood with her nose inches from the oak, smile fixed, the whitening knuckles on her tablet the only sign of her reaction. Then she took a deep breath and muttered, "Sodding javerzaharses. How'd you like to be shark bait?"

She turned and marched back toward the stairs, Kai ghosting along at her heels. Because really, her sotto voce commentary was telling. Not as telling as a quick word with Radka would be, but telling nonetheless.

"Beware of bridezillas, they said. Ha! Bridesmaids with delusions of event planning expertise are worse."

She touched an earpiece. "Smith? It's a no-go on the canned music." She rounded the elaborate bannister and stomped down the stairs. "I know, I know. But Sharkbait played the satisfaction-guaranteed card." She reached the entryway and stopped so quickly that Kai nearly ran into her. "The broom closet? Why are they heading there? If there's some kind of spill, Hazel's housekeeping team can take care of it."

Ah. Jovan must be taking them to Ole. As Kai raced back up the stairs, the last thing he heard her say was, "Know where I can get a live goat?"

When he reached the corridor leading to the groom's wing, Jovan was standing outside the broom closet door with two men in EO outfits. Kai reached them, out of breath, just as Jovan grasped the handle.

Jovan's head shot up. "Kai?"

"Yeah. I'm here."

The two EO men exchanged glances, and although they couldn't look more different—one tall, dark, and obviously Greek; the other as blond and blue-eyed as Radka's indistinguishable bridesmaids with *Norse* written all over him—their expressions of polite inquiry were identical.

"Do we...have the pleasure of another guest?"

Jovan nodded curtly. "Mikos, Anders, this is Kai. He's Radka's best friend."

"Of course. She's spoken about you. Klabautermann?" The blond man held out a hand. "Just call me Andy."

It wasn't often anyone offered to touch Kai when he was invisible—Jovan and Radka were the only ones, in fact. Somehow, having Andy and then Mikos offer to shake his hand was...validating. "A pleasure." But when Jovan held out his hand for Kai to hold, it was *more*.

As soon as Kai laced his fingers with his, Jovan's shoulders straightened and his head came up, as if having Kai there bolstered his own strength. Kai could relate—he hadn't felt *right* since Jovan left him at the Bellagio portal this morning.

"Have they seen Ole yet?" Kai murmured.

Jovan shook his head. "I had to check with him first. He's okay with both of them coming in. You too, obviously." He glared at Andy and Mikos, who must be made of stern stuff because neither one of them so much as flinched under Jovan's glower, amped up to eleven as it was. "He's trusting you to help him. If I see so much as a hint of judgment..." Jovan let the threat hang in the air.

Mikos's level gaze didn't waver. "We're not here to cast blame—"

"Or throw shade," Andy added.

"Whatever the problem is, we'll fix it. That's what we do."

Jovan's grip tightened on Kai's hand, but he nodded, then rapped on the door with one knuckle. "Ole? We're coming in now."

"Okay." Ole's voice wavered a bit. Poor guy must be so freaking uncomfortable.

Jovan cracked open the door and reached in to switch off the lights. He stood aside and let Mikos and Andy enter first. "Mind the"—a muffled curse followed a clang and clatter— "mops."

Jovan eased in, but Kai held back. "Are you sure? It's gonna be pretty crowded in there."

"I'm sure." Jovan heaved a sigh. "Ole needs me. But I need you."

Well, that put a much rosier glow on things, didn't it? "Of course. Anything for you."

They slipped inside, much to the confusion of a passing sylph. *This probably looks like a weird inversion of a clown car, or a re-staging of the stateroom scene from that Marx Brothers movie.* They jostled for position, and Kai found himself with his back pressed against Jovan's chest. *Guess there are some bright spots to this disaster.*

"I'm about to turn on the lights, Ole," Jovan rumbled. "You ready?"

"Uh huh."

Jovan flicked the switch, revealing Ole cowering on his bucket, blinking in the light.

"Odin's beard," Andy muttered.

CHAPTER SEVEN

Jovan immediately blocked Andy's view of Ole. "I warned you—"

"No, no. Please don't misunderstand. I'm not judging, I'm just *empathizing.*" He edged around Jovan, although it wasn't easy to do in the close confines of the closet. "Ole, that looks so *painful.*"

Ole shrugged. "It was worse when it was, you know, *happening.*"

"Well, we'll get you set to rights. Smith, our tech demon, knows a witch-doctor—"

"He's a doctor-witch, I believe, Andy," Mikos murmured.

Andy waved one hand. "Same difference. We can get him here *tout de suite,* but..." Andy bit his lip. "I have to ask—and I promise, no judgment—what do you want him to do? Do you want him to soothe your skin or grow your fur back?"

"Well..." Ole plucked at the sleeve of his robe. "If Radka likes—"

"Fur," Kai said. "Definitely the fur. Radka fell in love with Ole's true self. She'd never expect him to change his nature for her."

Ole blinked up at them. "Really?"

"Yes, really," Kai said. "I told you. She loves your fur."

Ole set his chin—which wasn't nearly as prominent when he looked like a giant naked mole rat who'd had a run in with a swarm of hornets. "Then I want my fur back."

Andy nodded decisively and Mikos hummed low in his throat, which set up an odd resonance that caused the jars on the shelves to judder. Andy jabbed Mikos in the side with an elbow and the humming stopped, although Mikos's cheeks flared pink. *Oh right. Radka told me. He's half siren.*

Andy smiled brightly. "We'll get you fixed up, although I can't guarantee it won't be uncomfortable."

"It can't be worse than I feel right now," Ole said glumly.

"Okay then. It'll probably also take some time. We'll need to push the ceremony back"—Andy squinted up at the ceiling—"I'm guessing a couple of hours, although we'll know more after Dr. Makori takes a look at you." He stood up and faced his boss. "I'd suggest we get the cocktail buffet set up now."

Mikos winced. "Are you sure?"

"This day is about Ole and Radka, and if the guests have to wait awhile, that's a price I'm willing to pay. But nothing soothes impatient people like food and free booze." He took a deep breath. "Are you going to tell him, or should I?"

Jovan scowled at them. "Tell who what?"

Andy grimaced. "Our chef is a little, um, temperamental. He might object a bit to having his timetable thrown off—and possibly having to expand the buffet to last several hours instead of one."

"I'll go," Mikos said.

Andy glanced up at him worriedly. "Are you sure?"

"Yes. You stay here and wait for Dr. Makori."

"Do you need the motorcycle helmet? The Kevlar suit? The flamethrower?"

"Kevlar suit?" Kai murmured, his breath ghosting along on Jovan's cheek, sending a shiver down his spine. "Flamethrower?"

Mikos shot a tight smile toward the source of Kai's voice. "Chef is a goblin berserker."

Fuck. Goblin berserkers made Úlfheðinn like Jovan look like baby unicorns.

"Ah." Jovan heard Kai's nervous gulp. "Say no more."

Mikos returned his attention to Andy. "I'll take the flower fairy Incident Response Team with me. They can always calm Chef down. If worse comes to worst?" He shrugged. "I can always sing." He nodded at Jovan and to the air next to Jovan's shoulder. "A pleasure, gentlemen. If you'll excuse me." He slipped out the door.

Andy smiled brightly at them and rubbed his palms together. "Alrighty then. Jovan, if you could check the corridor to make sure the coast is clear, we'll whisk Ole into his dressing room to wait for Dr. Makori. I'll have Brooke announce the change in agenda to the guests—"

"I, um, think she might be a little busy," Kai said. "She's trying to find a goat."

Andy's eyebrows shot up. "A goat?"

"And enough water from Ofotfjord." Jovan felt Kai shrug. "To fill a marble bathtub."

Andy closed his eyes. "I don't even want to know." When he opened his eyes again, he set his jaw in a decidedly mulish fashion that Jovan recognized very well

—he saw the same expression on his own face in the mirror when he was prepping for a challenging job. "In that case, Jovan, I'll have to ask you, as best man, to take over the task. Once the guests have arrived and we've herded—I mean escorted them into the banquet hall, will you stand in for Ole? Keep everyone happy?"

Jovan lifted an eyebrow. "I'm not sure I've ever kept anyone happy in my life."

"Oh, I wouldn't say that," Kai murmured, his voice laced with wicked suggestion. *Damn it.* Now Jovan's dick was perking up.

"Well, if you can't keep them happy, I have no doubt you can keep them in line."

Jovan nodded. "That I can do." He glanced down at his clothes. Kai had done a decent job ironing them—another surge of heat shot through Jovan—but they weren't exactly pristine. "I should probably change, though."

Andy nodded. "That would be best. Your tux is laid out in the room next door. I don't think you'll have an opportunity later, since we'll want to herd, I mean *escort* the guests directly into the chapel as soon as Ole is ready."

"Right." Jovan gazed down at Ole. "Don't worry, buddy. We've got your back."

Ole smiled wanly. "I know. Thanks, Jovan."

Jovan squeezed Kai's fingers. "You're best suited for stealthy reconnaissance. Want to check if the coast is clear?"

"Why do I feel like I'm being used, and not in the fun way?"

Behind them, Andy snorted, but Kai released Jovan's hand and a moment later, the door cracked open.

"All clear," Kai whispered and held the door wide so Andy and Jovan could hustle Ole three doors down the hall and into his dressing room.

Jovan was about to shut the door on Andy and Ole when Kai's hand landed on his arm. "Just a minute." Kai brushed past Jovan, standing close enough that Jovan could feel his heat. "Andy, I meant to tell you. I think Taline and the other bridesmaids are up to something."

"What more can they do?" Jovan growled. "Wasn't ripping Ole's fur out by the roots enough?"

Ole whimpered. Andy started to pat him on the shoulder, but clearly thought better of it. "Thanks for the heads-up. They've been...a challenge throughout this whole process." He chuckled. "I'm afraid Taline will never forgive us for being in charge of the wedding instead of her."

"She seems to be doing her best to scuttle the ship," Kai grumbled.

Andy grinned. "Well, as long as you're still invisible, we know she hasn't succeeded."

Kai's surprised laugh vibrated Jovan's bones. "I guess you're right."

Jovan backed out the door, holding it open wide enough that Kai hopefully accompanied him. "We'll leave you to it then. Ole's got my number, so please text me if you need anything."

Andy's grin widened as he shooed them out of the room. "Don't worry. We'll have everything sorted in a twinkling of a wyvern's eye, just you wait and see."

"I hope he's right," Kai said as Jovan closed the door. "I couldn't get in to speak to Radka, and the expression on Taline's face... Brrr!"

Jovan tugged Kai toward his dressing room. "I'm sure they know what they're doing. Now come on. If I have to get dressed in the monkey suit and be *nice* to people, I need backup."

"Why, Agent Kos, are you admitting a weakness?"

Jovan's belly tumbled. *I've got a weakness all right, and you're it.* But his own inconvenient *feelings* aside, he wasn't lying. This wedding was stressing him out more than his toughest assignments. The look on Ole's face. *Loki's balls, Ole's poor* face. If this weren't Ole's wedding day, and if the proceedings hadn't been disrupted enough, Jovan would have hauled that Taline witch in on cross-species assault charges.

"Jovan?" Kai's voice took on a worried note. "I'm sorry. I didn't mean anything by that. I—"

"In here." Jovan yanked his dressing room door open, hauled Kai inside, then kicked the damn thing closed. The room was dim, with blackout shades covering the windows and the lights out. To make the darkness complete, Jovan closed his eyes, because in the dark, he could *feel* Kai, sense his presence, without his sight protesting that he was alone.

In the dark, his hands shaped Kai's waist, his chest, his face. Jovan threaded his hands through Kai's hair—shaggy, silky, and just begging for his grip—and brought their lips within a breath of one another. "I can face down rioting ghouls, gangs of biker trolls, a whole clan of Nibelungen in the throes of gold lust, but playing host to a bunch of Pures on a high-class bender is beyond my skill set." He kissed Kai, slow and deep, and was rewarded by a moan. "You may have noticed that I'm not exactly a people person." When Kai chuckled, Jovan was able to call up the image behind his eyelids. *Beautiful.*

"I've heard rumors to that effect, usually with the purveyor of said rumor glancing over their shoulder with the whites of their eyes showing."

"Some of those rumors are probably true."

"Some?" Kai said against Jovan's throat, and Jovan shivered.

"Most. Okay, maybe all. But that's why I need you with me."

"You realize they won't be able to see me. Neither will you."

"I know." Jovan sucked another mark on Kai's neck. *Where no one will know about it but us.* "But with you there, like an angel on my shoulder, reminding me to be nice and that putting Baba Lenka in a headlock would be a bad thing, I can handle it."

With you by my side, I could handle anything.

As much as Kai wanted to stay with Jovan and canoodle a little more in the dimness, unease still crept like frost ants up his spine. There was a reason he never hooked up in the Interstices: It was damned disorienting not to be able to see your own body. Half the thrill of sex was the sight of his own hands on another man's skin, watching the way they fit together, the sight of someone's —Jovan's—cock disappearing into him. It lost a little of the magic when the other guy's cock seemed to vanish the instant it entered Kai's mouth or…elsewhere. More than one partner had shrieked like a bean sidhe and bolted from the tryst, sometimes without bothering to locate their pants.

Yeah, thinking your dick had been removed by your lover was a real mood-killer.

So Kai reluctantly stepped away from Jovan. "I want to try getting to Radka once more. Let her know to watch out for Taline."

"Surely the EO staff will tell her."

"They'll tell her about Ole, of course, and about the change in schedule, but about Taline's spitefulness?" Kai ran his hands up Jovan's chest and couldn't resist undoing a couple of buttons. *Totally legit—he has to change his clothes, anyway.*

"Radka's smart. She probably figured that out months ago, which is why she and Ole hired Enchanted Occasions." Jovan scowled, and Kai wanted to plant a kiss right in the middle of it. "Taline just assumed she'd be handling it. Hel, she'd already booked a venue in the Fiji Interstices if you can believe it. Fiji! Ole would have been more miserable there than he was in that damn bar last night."

Kai huffed a sigh. "He probably wishes he could turn back the clock and be back there now, considering his current state. I suspect he'd make different choices."

"I'd hope so." Jovan continued unbuttoning his shirt. *So distracting.* "But Ole's the most modest, soft-hearted guy in the Nine Worlds. He'd probably let himself get talked into it again, if—"

"If he thought Radka wanted it." Kai eased further away until he couldn't feel the heat of Jovan's skin as he slipped out of his shirt.

"Where'd you go?" Jovan reached for him, but Kai dodged to the side. "Come back. We've got a couple of hours before we have to show up and play host, and I have some ideas about how we can spend the time."

Jovan waggled his eyebrows in the worst attempt at a seductive leer that Kai had ever seen, but it warmed him from his toes to his forehead. *He doesn't get much practice.* And *that* was something Kai intended to hold on to, even if he and Jovan never saw each other—or rather if Jovan never saw *him*—again except as Ole and Radka's friends.

"I have to try to talk to her, Jovan. I'll have a better chance now than if I wait until closer to the ceremony. I'll be back as soon as I can. I promise."

Jovan dropped his let's-have-sex expression, but his face didn't settle into his normal glower. He looked... sad, and it punched Kai right in the heart. "All right. But hurry back. I *really* don't want to face the hordes without you."

"I'll be quick. I promise."

But as it turned out, not only couldn't Kai get anywhere close to Radka—Taline was standing guard over her at the venue's spa suite like a blonde Cerberus—but when he tried to return to Jovan's dressing room, he got lost and ended up in the kitchens, where Mikos was calmly facing down an eight-foot-tall goblin berserker, made even taller by his white chef's toque, who was in full battle rage. That he was brandishing a cheese grater, a measuring cup, and a mandoline in three of his four arms instead of a sword, mace, or battle ax didn't make the showdown any less alarming.

Then he got trapped in the entry hall by a mass of guests waiting to sign the guest book and drink their required adaptation elixir. *That's one of the few advantages to being an aitcher.* The transition from Earthside to the Interstices didn't make him want to puke.

When he got to the groom's wing again, the other groomsmen were milling around in the corridor, all looking decidedly worse for wear. None of them had changed into their tuxes yet. Kai stood outside Jovan's door for a moment, shifting from foot to foot. *Go into your dressing rooms already, you idiots.*

He smacked himself in his invisible forehead. *I don't need to hide my presence from them.* Chances are they wouldn't notice if a manticore galloped down the hall.

"Screw it," he muttered and opened the door to slip inside.

Jovan had opened the blinds, so the artificial sunlight of the Interstices streamed in through the windows. He was looking out of one of them, shirtless, his arms braced on the frame, and the muscles in his back, the way his biceps bulged, made Kai's mouth go dry. He had to swallow twice before he could speak.

"Jovan. It's me." Jovan's head snapped around and he focused on exactly where Kai was standing. "I'm sorry it took so long."

Jovan turned away from the window and Kai was treated to a full-on view of that deliciously hairy chest in bright sunlight. "Did you talk to her?"

"No." Kai had learned not to nod or shake his head in the Interstices. "I couldn't get anywhere close. Then I got trapped in the kitchen—"

"It's okay." Jovan sighed. "Guess I can't put it off any longer, eh?"

"I'm afraid not." Kai gave in to temptation and padded across the gleaming oak floor to slip his arms around Jovan's waist. "Time to face the public, Agent Kos. Your assignment awaits."

"Fuck," Jovan muttered, then he grinned down at Kai. *Wow.* Now *that* let's-have-sex expression was much more potent. "Kiss me. I need fortification if I'm going to get through this."

Kai was more than happy to oblige, fitting his mouth over Jovan's, since Jovan couldn't locate Kai's without some exploration. Which Kai didn't object to on principle, but they were on the clock now.

"Better get your shirt and jacket on." *Before I rip your pants off.*

"Fine."

And really, watching Jovan get into his tux—grousing all the while—was one of the highlights of Kai's year. Shit, maybe his entire life. Jovan was mouthwatering naked. That sight would always be number one in Kai's mental scrapbook.

But Jovan in a tux... *Rawr.*

"Damned bow tie," Jovan growled, yanking it off for the fourth time. "Why can't I—"

"Let me have it." Kai tugged at the mangled fabric. "You have to let go of it first."

"Sorry." Jovan peered at the mirror to watch the tie seemingly float into a perfect knot of its own accord. "You're good at that."

Kai gave the tie one final tweak. "Well, I get a lot of practice Earthside. My station either hosts or participates in a lot of charity events." He chuckled. "Although I must admit this is the first time I've tied one in the Interstices."

"Why?" Jovan's brows drew together. "Don't people invite you because you're an aitcher?"

"That's not the reason." Although his Interstitial invitations *were* pretty minimal. Hosting an invisible guest was awkward enough, but if that invisible guest suddenly popped into view? Nobody wanted their party to turn into a proven disaster. Without the evidence of a Klabautermann sighting, they could at least maintain plausible deniability. "But in case you hadn't noticed, I'm not naked."

Jovan's forehead cleared. "Come here. I need to check."

Laughing, Kai dodged Jovan's wandering hands. "Not a chance, Agent Kos. You've got hosting duties awaiting you."

"Ugh. Don't remind me."

"The reason is because anything I wear or carry becomes invisible too. Caught in my transparency matrix. Although I can tie a regular necktie by touch, I've never been able to manage a bow tie." He patted Jovan's arm. "Now, are you ready for your closeup?"

Jovan held out his hand. "You won't leave me?"

At the plaintive note in Jovan's growl, Kai's heart made that odd sideways thump again. *Damn it. Do not fall in love with him.* Kai suspected that particular order was already doomed to failure—like closing the stable door after the gryphon had already flown.

He took Jovan's hand. "I promise. Now let's get this over with. By the end of the day, Ole and Radka will be married and all of this will be behind us."

"Right." Jovan tilted his head in an alarming crack of his neck. "Let's do this."

He charged across the room, towing Kai along with him, and threw open the door. The groomsmen weren't in the corridor anymore, but Andy was just topping the stairs at a trot.

"Oh, there you are." He smiled at them sunnily. "We're ready for you in the banquet hall now."

"How's Ole?" Jovan asked.

"Coming along nicely." Andy's smile grew a little fixed. "It's a sort of…" He sketched a motion in the air. "…top-down process. We're about at chin level now."

"Chin level," Kai said, earning a blink from Andy. "In two hours? How will he be fully refurred by the ceremony?"

Andy smiled kindly in Kai's direction. "It took some time to set the spell up. It will continue to work until Ole's fur is completely regrown. But for the ceremony, we only have to make sure the parts visible outside his wedding doublet will be finished. The rest can continue under his clothing." Andy grimaced. "He might be uncomfortable. A little itchy. But Dr. Makori assures me the spell will be complete by the time Ole and Radka depart for their honeymoon."

Kai heaved a sigh of relief. "Thank goodness." At least Ole wouldn't have to face Radka on their wedding night looking like a sea urchin without its shell.

"Let's go." Andy—who seemed to have only one default speed—zoomed back toward the stairs. Jovan had no trouble keeping up with his longer legs, but Kai had to run or be left behind. "Chef has the buffet all set up, and the bartenders are ready to serve. I'll announce you, and you can make your entrance."

Jovan's eyes rounded. "I won't have to make a speech, will I?"

"No, no. I'll handle that." Andy chuckled as he skidded to a stop outside the banquet hall's vast doors. "Trust me, they'll be thrilled to see you. Chef won't let them get near the food until you arrive."

Kai leaned in and kissed Jovan's neck. "Don't worry. You've got this."

"I hope you're right," he muttered.

Andy threw open the doors with a flourish and marched inside. "Honored guest, I present to you—"

"Radka! Darling!"

Jovan froze, his hand tightening on Kai's, as somebody pawed at the velvet drapes on the opposite side of the room. "That's not Ole's voice."

"No." Kai said around clenched teeth as a tall, white-blond light elf in a fricking *wedding doublet* finally fought his way free of the drapes. "It's Torvald."

CHAPTER EIGHT

Torvald? Radka's ex? Jovan grabbed Andy's elbow. "What the Hel is he doing here?"

To his credit, Andy didn't flinch. In fact, the expression on his face rivaled Jovan's best—or worst, depending on your point of view—scowl. "I don't know. But he was definitely not invited."

Torvald strutted forward, his arms stretched wide as if he were embracing the whole crowd. *But not Radka. Not if I have anything to do with it.* Ole had told Jovan about Radka's first husband, not that he had to go into a lot of detail. All light elves were arrogant assholes.

"Friends," Torvald warbled, "dearest family, have no fear. I've returned and you have nothing more to worry about." His dismissive gaze flicked over the guests who were obviously from Ole's side, his lip lifting in a sneer when his gaze landed on Uncle Snorre. To be fair, Uncle Snorre was looking decidedly worse for wear, and the draugr stench clashed with the delectable aromas wafting from the buffet table.

Damn it. Snorre probably forgot his anti-scent charms again, even though he'd promised Ole faithfully that he'd pack extras. None of the commercially available spells were very effective against…well…death.

Torvald wrapped an arm around Baba Lenka, who, if she wasn't wearing the same outfit as last night, was wearing an identical one—black, black, and more black, accessorized by a knitted shawl that had more holes than yarn. "Baba Lenka, you haven't aged a day." He planted a kiss on her apple-doll forehead and she, by Odin, *simpered* at him.

"Shit, Jovan," Kai whispered. "The whole pack of them are sabotaging the wedding on purpose. Radka's family never really accepted the divorce."

Torvald turned his back on Ole's family—a mistake, considering Ole's cousin Solveig was a Valkyrie and was studying Torvald with an expression that made Jovan check her hand for her sword. "Radka, my love, I'm here. We're together again in the bosom of your family. We can —" He frowned, peering around at the crowd. "Where's Radka?"

Jovan strode through the crowd and gripped Torvald by the arm. "She's not here. And you shouldn't be here either."

Baba Lenka squawked and batted at Jovan with the tail of her shawl, but Jovan ignored her and towed Torvald toward the door. "Outside." He lost Kai's hand in the process, but trusted him to know the *Outside* comment was aimed at him too.

Andy appeared next to Jovan's elbow. "Get him into the entryway. Mikos will take it from there."

"Got it."

"Unhand me, you... you..." Torvald finally took a good look at Jovan, and his already pale skin blanched further. "Jovan Kos?" he squeaked.

"The same. I don't know what the Hel you think you're doing—"

"I'm saving my darling Radka from a fate worse than death." Torvald's long white-blond hair flipped sideways. "Ow!" He rubbed his head. "What— Who—"

"That's for Radka, you douchebucket," Kai muttered. And judging by Torvald's squawk and the way his head jerked forward, Kai had probably smacked him again.

"Everything's fine, folks," Andy called. "Please help yourself to a libation or two and enjoy the buffet." The doors boomed shut behind them. "Whew!"

Torvald yanked his arm out of Jovan's grip. "You may be an ILE agent, Kos, but you're still a Jötunn. You can't possibly think a *goblin* is a fit mate for a beautiful woman like Radka. He has a *snout*, for Odin's sake."

"It's not a snout. He's got a snub nose," Kai said hotly, making Torvald glance around wildly. "And Radka *loves* Ole's face. She says it has *character*."

Torvald snorted. "That's one way to put it. Only people who can never claim beauty fall back on character." He straightened his doublet with its over-the-top gold embroidery. "Tell Radka I'm here. She'll come to her senses when she sees me again."

"If Radka sees you again, she'll launch a whirlwind on your ass in a red-hot minute, you—"

A haunting melody wafted through the hall, and Torvald, who seemed ready to fling himself in the direction of Kai's voice, blinked, a blissful expression banishing his previous peevish one. He turned toward the source of the music, and Jovan spotted Mikos standing in a doorway under the stairs, his gaze riveted on Torvald as he sang.

As Torvald tottered away, Andy chuckled. "Mikos is getting really, really good at pinpointing his siren's song. Now." He glanced back at the doors, which were heavy enough to muffle any sounds from inside. "Ole may be ready to get into his own doublet by now. Let's go check in on him and get this wedding started before somebody else pops out of the woodwork.

As they headed toward the stairs, Brooke passed them leading a prancing baby goat dressed in pink kitten-print pajamas. She glanced at them and sighed. "Don't ask." An enormous troll shouldering a marble basin the size of a hot tub and a troop of brownies carting buckets of water followed her.

Andy watched the little parade enter the hall, his brow knotted in concern. He smiled up at Jovan apologetically. "I'd better check on her and make sure Mikos doesn't need any backup with Torvald too. Could you two go on up to Ole's dressing room? I'll meet you there in ten minutes, tops."

"Sure." Jovan held out his hand, and something remarkably like calm settled over him when Kai laced his fingers with his.

As they ascended the stairs, Kai murmured, "I wonder if Radka knows Torvald is here."

Jovan's head snapped around, and he glared at Kai's approximate location. "You think she *planned* to humiliate Ole this way?" he growled.

"What?" Kai said indignantly. "Of course not! She moved to Earthside Vegas to get *away* from that asshole. She's never been happier than since she met Ole."

Jovan pulled them to a stop at the top of the stairs and turned to face Kai's voice. "Then how the Hel did he end up here?"

A brownie in EO livery passing by with a stack of dripping empty buckets stared up at him with wide, startled eyes. "Who, sir?"

"Nobody," Jovan barked, then closed his eyes and took a breath. It wasn't the brownie's fault. "Sorry. Just a little stressed. Weddings. Am I right?"

"O-of course, sir," she said and scuttled down the hall with her buckets and opened the door of the broom cupboard.

Jovan huffed a breath, then realized that Kai's hand in his was vibrating. He squinted at the Kai-occupied air. "Are you laughing at me?"

"Sorry. I'm sorry. But watching you try to be *affable* is just so... so..."

"Hopeless? Ridiculous? Impossible?"

"I was going to say adorable."

Heat rushed up Jovan's throat. *Adorable?* "Nobody has ever accused me of being adorable before."

"Then nobody has been paying attention." Kai squeezed his fingers. "As far as who smuggled Torvald in for his grand entrance, I'd say we've got a number of suspects." He tugged Jovan forward, although he made sure they cut a wide berth around the EO brownie, who gave Jovan a decidedly nervous glance as she emerged from the broom cupboard.

"Taline," Jovan growled.

"Taline might have been part of the execution, but I don't think she was the instigator of the plan. She's an implementer, not a mastermind."

"Baba Lenka."

"High on the list, although it could be any one of Radka's more reactionary relatives. For that matter, she told me not all of Ole's family is in favor of the match either."

"Just the ones who object to the furless."

"So you see, lots of possibilities for the *who*, but that doesn't matter now, because it failed, right?"

"I suppose."

"Grumpy because you can't bust anyone's head?"

The feather touch on his cheek—*Kai's fingertips*—caused a shiver to skate down Jovan's spine. "Maybe."

"Hold that thought. We still have the ceremony and reception to get through, so who knows? You may yet get your chance."

Andy pounded down the corridor and slid to a stop next to them. "All sorted." He grinned at Jovan and managed to include Kai in his grin. "Brooke has things well in hand in the banquet hall."

"What about Torvald?" Kai asked.

"Oh, don't worry about him." He patted the air, and since his hand met resistance, Jovan assumed he'd located some part of Kai's anatomy. A growl rumbled in his chest and Andy glanced at him quizzically, but clearly misunderstood Jovan's reaction. "No, really. Torvald is taken care of. Chef put him on ice."

"Um... Taken care of?" Kai's uncertainty was clear in his tone. "On ice? You don't mean he's—"

Andy blinked, then broke out laughing. "Chef didn't *kill* him. He stashed him in the walk-in fridge."

"I'm not sure that's much better."

"He's got blankets, and Chef served him a three-course meal. He's a goblin berserker, not a *monster*." He patted them both this time. "Now, let's see how Ole's refurring is going and get him ready to greet his bride, shall we?"

The door of Ole's dressing room swung open and Ole stepped into the corridor. They could all tell exactly how well his refurring had progressed—from his head to the middle of his chest—because he was otherwise completely naked.

"Hi, guys," he said shyly. "I'm ready."

Beside him, Kai uttered a strangled gasp and Andy muttered, "Odin's beard."

"Not quite yet, big guy." Jovan let go of Kai and hustled Ole back into the dressing room. "You kind of need to put on some clothes first."

Ole gazed at Jovan, wide-eyed. "But I did." He peered down at himself. "Although it wasn't easy to put on the suit. I can understand the trouble Kai must have." He chuckled. "Handling invisible clothes isn't easy. You can't even *feel* them."

"Ole," Kai said. "I can feel my clothes. I just can't see them. And from what we can see and what I can feel"— the fur on Ole's biceps fluttered as though a finger had ruffled it—"you're not wearing anything at all."

The look on Ole's face when he realized he was naked in front of them—that he'd almost walked into his own wedding naked—nearly broke Kai's heart.

"But— But it's a wind-colored doublet and hose," Ole moaned as Jovan helped him back into his robe. "To match Radka's dress." He shot a pleading look at Andy.

"The Enchanted Occasions spells makes wind-colored garments visible to everyone, not just vila. Right?"

"Ole," Andy said gently. "There's no such thing as wind-colored clothing."

Kai had seen Radka's dress, and it was most definitely white—he'd helped her pick it out, an exact replica of Princess Leia's gown during the last scene of *A New Hope.*

Ole sank down onto a damask wingback chair and dropped his head into his hands, which were now dotted with the tips of newly sprouting fur, although the fur was growing in auburn, not silver. "She said it was beautiful. More beautiful than Torvald's was for Radka's first wedding. I thought the only reason I couldn't see it was because I'm a... you know..."

"Who said it?" Jovan growled.

"Taline." He pointed to a garment bag, sagging empty on the valet stand. "The bridesmaids gave it to me last night, before the, er, waxing."

Anger burned along Kai's veins, and for the first time, he understood what drove Jovan to track down cross-species crimes for the ILE, what might prompt him to go into his wolf-berserker rage. "Ole. They gave you an empty garment bag."

"But why?" Ole looked up at them, his big brown eyes bleak. "All I want is for Radka to be happy. Surely that's what her friends and family want too."

Jovan gripped Ole's shoulder. "Not everyone is as altruistic, buddy. But you know what? Nobody matters but you and Radka. You still want to marry her, right?"

Ole narrowed his eyes, and for the first time since Kai had met him, he looked like a textbook menacing goblin. "You really have to ask that?"

Jovan lifted an eyebrow. "No. Not if you were willing to take a wind-colored outfit on faith, not to mention get a full body wax just to keep her happy. So what do you say we get you dressed in your *real* wedding doublet and get the two of you hitched?"

Panic chased across Ole's face. "I don't have another outfit. I gave it to Taline in exchange for this one, and she handed it over to somebody at the spa."

Jovan shot Andy a disgusted look. "What are the odds she actually brought it with her."

Andy lifted his palms in a shrug. "Somewhere from none to a negative three thousand and two?"

"I don't think odds work that way," Ole murmured. "But it doesn't matter because I still don't have anything to wear. I can't very well get married in this robe."

"You can borrow my suit," Kai said, and then winced. "Except it's not big enough. Damn it. Sorry."

Andy perked up. "No, it's okay. Our staff magicians can morph it into a ringer for Ole's wedding doublet."

Jovan scowled—what a surprise. "Why not just use the robe, then?"

To Andy's credit, he didn't lose his smile when faced with Jovan's rather accusatory tone. "Because the robe isn't *intended* to be something worn to a wedding. Kai's suit—" He turned to Kai, hope written all over his face. "Your suit is wedding appropriate, right? Trousers, shirt, jacket, tie?"

"Yeah." Kai drew out the word.

Andy clapped his hands. "Perfect!" He glanced around the room. "Where is it?"

Jovan smacked his forehead. "It's invisible too, right? So that won't work."

Kai punched Jovan in the arm on his way past. "It's only invisible on me or when I'm carrying it. I left it..." Damn, where *had* he left it? He'd shown up in response to Jovan's distress call and run upstairs to the... "The broom cupboard. I hung it on one of the shelf units."

"Good." Andy darted for the door. "Let's hope the brownies on the housekeeping staff didn't move it out of an excess of efficiency.

All of them—including Ole—started to follow Andy, but Jovan stopped Ole with a hand on his chest. "You wait here. We'll be back."

Ole nodded, although Kai's last sight of him as Jovan closed the door was decidedly forlorn.

Damn Taline. Damn Baba Lenka. Damn them all. Kai was surprised the steam coming out his ears didn't leave a contrail in his wake. Why couldn't Radka's family keep their noses—and mean-spirited tricks—out of Radka's business?

Andy threw open the broom cupboard door, and a grin split his face. "It's here! Thank Freya." He zipped inside and returned with Kai's garment bag. "This will delay things a bit more," he said, glancing from Jovan to the empty hallway. *Probably trying to locate me.* "Ole will have to be isolated with the magicians and the suit, so I'll have to ask you to stay out of the dressing room until they're done."

"No problem," Jovan said, then tugged at his collar. "Uh... I won't have to go play host again, will I?"

Andy patted his arm. "No, no. The guests should be occupied with eating and drinking for a while, plus Brooke and Mikos are on the job. You can join them if you like." He winked. "I imagine you could use a drink by now."

"Thanks." Jovan's gaze slid away from Andy to Kai's precise location. "I'll consider it."

"Excellent." Andy draped the garment bag over his arm. "And Kai, thank you again. You've saved the day— or at least Ole's dignity."

He zipped away and disappeared into Ole's dressing room.

Kai turned to Jovan. "Well, I guess we can— Eeep!"

Jovan's big arm snaked unerringly around Kai's waist and pulled him into the broom cupboard. His smile was positively wicked, and it sent all kinds of delicious tremors through Kai's body. "I've got better things to do than raise a glass with that bunch of sneaky, vindictive harpies."

"There you go, dissing harpies again," Kai said shakily. "They might relish a little vindictiveness, but don't tar them with the 'sneaky' brush. As a species, they're much more direct."

"Well, I'm pretty direct myself." Jovan reached over and flipped the lights off.

"Jovan. It's, um, dark."

"I know." Jovan's hands, big and warm and wonderful, cupped Kai's face. "In the dark, I can see you perfectly."

Then, stars and storms, Jovan's lips were on Kai's. Teasing, tasting, worshipping. So gentle for such a powerful man. But while Kai appreciated the solicitude, he wanted more, so he pulled away with a gasp.

"Jovan, I'm invisible. Not *fragile*."

Jovan's chuckle vibrated Kai's bones. "I know. But I also know that you deserve as much consideration as Ole. As

Radka. And I may do a shit job of being caring and compassionate—"

"You don't. I mean, you *are* caring and compassionate. You just show it differently. Sometimes with excessive force."

Jovan sighed and leaned his forehead against Kai's. "I don't know how this is going to work, Kai. You've got a job you love—"

"Well, I've got a job," Kai said wryly.

"And so do I. More than that, I've got a vocation. There are rules attached to being an ILE agent. Restrictions. Some things I can never reveal except in extreme, life-altering circumstances."

Kai stroked Jovan's cheek. "I know. I would never ask you—"

"No, you don't get it." Jovan's voice was tight, almost as if he were in pain. "*This* is a life-altering circumstance."

"Hiding in a broom cupboard?"

Jovan uttered a strangled laugh. "No. I mean *you*. You altered my life. I think I fell in love with you two years ago, on that second movie night at Ole's place in Niflheim."

"Jovan, we were watching a *Nightmare on Elm Street* marathon. And you wouldn't have been able to see me. Which was a good thing, since I was hiding my eyes behind my fingers the whole time."

"It didn't matter. I could tell by what you said, by how kind you were, by what you laughed at." Jovan groaned and took Kai's lips in a bruising kiss. *Much better!* "Loki's balls, Kai, your laugh. Especially that little chuckle. It just slays me."

Kai laced his fingers behind Jovan's neck. "I doubt that any of your acquaintances would believe you appreciate a good laugh, let alone that it turns you on."

"Not anyone's laugh. Just yours." He kissed Kai's temple. "And then when I finally saw you yesterday, finally *kissed* you. I knew that was it for me. I was doomed. Doomed to love you forever."

Kai's throat closed and he could barely croak, "Jovan."

"What I'm saying is..." Jovan's shoulders rose and fell under Kai's arms. "What I'm saying is that I want to find a way for us to work. That is... I mean, if you feel anything like the same. And if you don't, I won't blame you. I'm Úlfheðinn. A wolf berserker. A beast. You could have—"

Kai stopped Jovan's ridiculous words with his mouth, moaning into the kiss, at the decadent slide of tongues and mingling of breath. When they came up for more air —far too soon, in Kai's opinion—he managed to croak, "Yes."

"Yes?"

"Yes, I feel the same way." He chuckled—and so maybe it was on purpose, but it worked, because Jovan's possessive growl in response was *everything*. "I think I might have fallen in love with you when you made that special vegetable dish for Ole the first night, because his family had been after him for his vegetarianism again."

Jovan squeezed Kai tight, and it was *perfect*. "So you think we could—"

The door banged open. "Ole, are you in here? Radka is *waiting*," someone said in a peevish tone.

The lights flicked on. Kai blinked in the glare and suddenly somebody was shrieking, a seesaw keening like a London police siren.

It's not me, and it's not Jovan. Kai finally managed to squint through the brightness. Ice Pink bridesmaid was standing in the door, pointing at them, her mouth stretched wide in an Edvard Munch-worthy scream.

The anger that had been building in Kai all day, with every dig at Ole and Radka, every attempt to derail their happiness, finally boiled over because, damn it, Jovan was *not* a beast, and nobody, let alone some insipid blonde toady, got to treat him this way.

"Can it, whoever you are. You show him some respect or I swear I'll—"

"Kai. Babe." Jovan's voice held apprehension and a bit of awe. "She's not pointing at me. She's pointing at you."

"Me?" Kai glanced down at himself. Black jeans. Blue T-shirt. Gray blazer. "Holy crap. I'm *visible.*" He turned to Jovan, icy panic dousing the fire of his Jovan-induced arousal. "I have to leave. Immediately."

"Why?" Jovan grimaced and shot a murderous glower at Ice Pink. "Shut the Hel up or I'll have you up on noise pollution charges."

For a wonder, she obeyed. Well, maybe not so much a wonder. Jovan's glower was amped up to about a hundred now. She snapped her mouth shut, hiked up her skirts, and bolted.

Kai moaned, clutching Jovan's lapels and peering up into his face. "She's bound to tell everybody. As soon as she spreads the news of a Klabautermann sighting, everyone will know."

Jovan, now that Ice Pink's air-raid siren effects were gone, wasn't glowering anymore. He was gazing down at Kai, a soft, almost fond, smile playing on his lips. He trailed a finger along Kai's cheekbone. "You're so gorgeous."

Kai grabbed Jovan's shoulders and tried to shake him, which of course accomplished the square root of nothing. "You don't understand. I'm *visible*."

"I noticed." He leaned down for a kiss, but Kai blocked him with a hand over his mouth.

"Jovan. A Klabautermann is only visible when the ship is about to sink."

"We're not on a ship."

"No. We're at Ole and Radka's wedding." Kai let go of Jovan and clutched his hair. "Damn, I said that Taline was trying to scuttle the ship. Obviously she's succeeded."

Jovan's brows snapped together. "Wait. You think the wedding is doomed?"

"What else?"

"I thought it was just me. Doomed to love you."

Kai propped his hands on his hips. "That kind of doom isn't *fatal*."

"Depends on your point of view." An absolutely sappy smile ambushed Jovan's scowl and Kai stamped his foot.

What am I doing? I never *stamp my foot.* "Why are you smiling? This is serious."

"I can't help it. I can see you. It's...distracting. You're cute when you're angry."

"I'm not angry, I'm terrified." He paced to the door. "Something must have happened since we came in here. Something that threatens the wedding. I have to get out of here right now, or who knows what will happen? Something more to Ole? Something to Radka? To both of them? If I don't leave, they'll never get their happy ever after, and we promised, Jovan. We *vowed* we'd make it happen. You and me."

Jovan's expression turned resolute. "You're right. We need to find out what's going on."

"You need to. I need to leave." Kai whirled, but Jovan caught his arm before he could bolt out the door.

"Kai. From everything I know about Klabautermänner, you don't *cause* the ship to sink."

"No, of course not." Kai tugged ineffectually at Jovan's grip. "We're committed to the ship, to its crew. We *help* when we can."

"So your appearance now isn't causing whatever this looming disaster might be. It just presages it. It's a warning." Jovan shifted his grip to Kai's hand. "And if we're warned, we can *do* something."

Kai let himself be pulled out of the broom cupboard. "Like what?"

"I don't know. But you said your father saved your mom from drowning, right?"

"Yeah."

"So let's make sure Ole and Radka don't drown." He strode down the corridor toward the balcony. "As for the rest of those jokers, they can all sink like fucking bricks for all I care." He stopped and faced Kai. "If things are about to get worse, I'm going to need your help. Are you with me?"

Kai took a deep breath and nodded once. "Always."

Jovan kissed him, quick and hot. "Then let's do this."

CHAPTER NINE

Jovan nearly took a header down the stairs—twice—because he couldn't tear his eyes away from Kai. The way the candlelight from the enormous chandelier picked out the gold in his brown hair. His lithe grace as he navigated the stairs. The little worry wrinkle between his brows and how he shoved his glasses further onto the bridge of his nose with one knuckle.

He did all those things, was all those things from the moment we met. But until last night, Jovan had never seen them before. After last night, he'd accepted—more or less—that his glimpses of Kai would be few and far between, but now he wasn't sure he could endure that kind of torture.

I need to see him every day. Touch him every day. Kiss him every day. The only question—well, one of many—in Jovan's mind now that they'd both admitted their feelings, was how to accomplish it. The ILE vows bound his tongue as well as his actions. He literally *couldn't* tell Kai about his nature unless he wanted to be struck mute until ILE Internal Affairs took it into their thick skulls to lift the spell and interrogate him. Since he wasn't especially popular with eighty percent of the ILE brass—including the IA goons—he could be kicking his heels for days. Weeks. Months, if he couldn't expedite matters with some judicious reminders of the goons' own past indiscretions.

There are exceptions. I know there are. I just can't remember any of them now. He'd never expected to run into any personally, so he'd never paid attention to the details.

But as he caught himself yet again because the light cast an alluring shadow under Kai's cheekbones, he made a vow to himself: He'd check out all the fine print. Ask for special dispensation.

And if that doesn't work? Would he, could he resign from ILE? Abandon his life's calling?

He glanced at Kai again and caught him peering up at him with an anxious frown. *Yes. For him, I would.* There would be other ways to serve, to protect the supernatural races from each other. But there would never be another Kai.

"Jovan?" Kai tugged him to a stop at the foot of the stairs. "Are you okay? You seem a little…distracted."

Jovan threaded his fingers through Kai's hair, fascinated by the way the strands slipped through his fingers. "I'll cop to that." He smiled down into Kai's worried face. "It's all your fault."

He frowned, and that cute worry wrinkle deepened. Jovan wanted to explore it with his tongue. "You just said I didn't *cause* the disaster—"

"Whoa, whoa, whoa." Jovan caught Kai's flailing hands. "I'm not blaming you for whatever caused you to become visible. Hel, whatever it is, I'm ready to celebrate it with a parade and fireworks. I just meant that I'm distracted because *you're* distracting. I've just never had the chance to ogle you in the Interstices before. I…" He rubbed the back of his neck. "I just didn't want to waste the opportunity."

Kai huffed an exasperated breath. "Jovan, what if the disaster is *you?*"

Jovan considered that for a minute. "I suppose that's not an unreasonable possibility. Most of the scumbags I apprehend think I'm worse than Ragnarok."

Kai rolled his eyes—*ungh! So adorable.* "I don't mean what if you *cause* the disaster. I mean what if something happens *to you?*"

"Nothing's going to happen to me."

"How do you know?" Kai pointed at the stairs. "You nearly tripped *three times.* What if you'd fallen and broken your neck? I..." He swallowed, his Adam's apple sliding beneath his golden skin. "I couldn't forgive myself."

"Okay." Jovan grinned and gave himself permission to smooth the brow wrinkle with one fingertip. "I'll admit my clumsiness was sort of your fault, since I can't stop looking at you."

"See?" Kai retreated out of Jovan's reach. *Not acceptable.* But when he tried to close the distance, Kai held up both hands, palms out. "I've been thinking. I told you Klabautermänner are committed to their ships, to the fate of the boat and its crew. But look around us." He flung his arms out.

To humor Kai, Jovan made a point of scanning the vast entry, the huge doors that led to the banquet hall, the bifurcated staircase, the lush tapestries lining the glistening faux-ice walls. "So?"

"So it's a *temporary construct.* The Enchanted Occasions magicians created this out of the Interstitial *nothingness* just for the wedding. A wedding I wasn't even supposed to be a part of. So why am I suddenly visible if the *wedding* is what's about to implode?"

Jovan frowned. "I'm not sure I follow."

Kai huffed again. "Jovan, I'm not committed to the *wedding*. I'm committed to *you*. What if... What if the doom I'm predicting is yours?"

Jovan's belly tumbled as though he really had missed his footing on the stairs. He held out a hand. "Kai. Come here?" Kai shook his head, crossing his arms, his full lips pressed together like a toddler refusing his peas. "Please? If what you're imagining is true—and I'm not saying it is —I want to hold you once more before we face it."

Kai set his chin mulishly, and Hel, even *that* was adorable. "We don't even know what *it* is."

"That's exactly my point." He beckoned. "Please?"

Kai let his hands fall to his sides. "How am I supposed to resist those puppy eyes?"

"I do *not* have puppy eyes," Jovan growled.

"You so do."

Jovan would have protested more, but since Kai moved closer and wrapped his arms around Jovan's waist, he was willing to let the insult go. He rested his cheek against Kai's silky hair. "Look at it this way. Your dad rescued your mom, right, even though the ship was sinking?"

"Yeah." Kai drew out the word, clearly suspicious.

"So the death and destruction wasn't complete."

"I suppose not."

"Besides..." Jovan pulled back so he could see Kai's face. *Never gonna get tired of that.* "I already told you. The doom is a done deal—I'm doomed to love you forever."

"Jovan," Kai said brokenly, his fists bunching in Jovan's tux jacket.

"Also, you're forgetting our vow."

Kai blinked up at him, his dark eyes glistening behind his glasses. "Our vow?"

"To make sure Ole and Radka get their happy ever after. You committed to that."

"You're right." Kai's expression cleared. "I did."

"Considering all the other shit that's been hitting this particular fan, I'd say the doom in question is probably waiting for us"—he jerked his chin at the banquet hall doors—"inside that room. Are you ready to face it with me?"

Kai stared at the doors with narrowed eyes. "Absolutely."

"Good." Jovan dropped a kiss on Kai's determined mouth, gentling the firm lips with his tongue until Kai opened for him with a moan. *I could do this all day.* But his tux wasn't tailored to accommodate an erection, and even without the obvious evidence of Kai's visibility, something was clearly about to go down. Jovan's Úlfheðinn instincts were hollering like a Valkyrie's battle cry.

So he reluctantly pulled away, with one final kiss to Kai's forehead. "Then let's see what we're facing."

He strode across the marble floor, Kai's hand in his more empowering than any weapon. But as they neared the door, Kai dropped behind and edged behind Jovan's shoulder. Jovan looked back at him.

"What are you doing?"

"I—" Kai blinked. "Oh. Sorry. Habit. When I'm invisible, I can't exactly lead the charge."

"Using me as a juggernaut again, eh?" Jovan said with a smirk.

"Hey, you're the one who volunteered Earthside."

"True. But for once, you don't have to step out of anybody's way."

Kai snorted. "When they see me, they'll probably fall over themselves to leap out of *my* way." He slanted a sly glance at Jovan. "Not that we'd notice. They do that around you all the time."

The return of Kai's cheeky attitude warmed Jovan to his bones—and to his boner too, unfortunately. But a discordant shriek from inside the hall, followed by a shout and a clatter, shocked him out of his lust haze.

"Was that a violin or a person?" Kai asked.

"Does it matter? Whatever it was, it's definitely our cue."

But as Jovan reached for the giant iron ring that passed for a doorknob, the doors burst open. He jumped back to avoid having his hand broken and something small, white, and furry—dressed in pink pajamas—galloped past him, bleating madly and trailing a frayed rope. Shouts and screams echoed from inside the room, which was a chaos of shifting bodies.

Kai stared after it. "Was that a goat? They're not trying to stage one of those weird Celtic rituals, are they?"

Suddenly, Brooke burst through the door, her blue tie askew and one pocket on her gray EO blazer ripped. Her moss-green hair was rumpled and her silver eyes wild. "They didn't tell me they were going to *sacrifice* the goat!" she wailed. "He's a *baby*. I only *borrowed* him from a goat yoga class in the Himalayan Interstices." The doors *whump*ed shut behind her, cutting off the noise. "Chef's about to go ballistic."

Jovan touched her shoulder as she ran past. "Is your Chef preparing raw goat for Uncle Snorre?"

"Who?" She shook her head. "No. It was that oh-so-famous Norse musician that Taline found." She backed away, practically vibrating with her obvious need to get away. "Sorry. I've got to find Andy and Mikos before this gets any worse."

She darted away as Jovan put two and two together. *Norse musician. Violin. Goat sacrifice.* Loki's balls... "I'm going to strangle Taline with my bare hands. She hired a bloody fossegrim."

"A what now?" Kai asked, although he was still peering after Brooke and the goat.

"A fossegrim. Norse water spirits and total pains in my ass. They're gifted violinists, brilliant teachers, but there's a catch if you want them to do anything for you."

"Wait." Kai clutched Jovan's sleeve. "Brooke said famous. Do you know of any famous fossegrims?"

Jovan just shrugged. "Only one. Knut." He snorted. "Arrogant SOB doesn't even cop to a last name."

"Knut." Kai spit out the name as if it were a mouthful of rotten fish. "Torvald cheated on Radka with a violinist named Knut. The asshole FedExed a goat heart to Radka at the station once, and that was *after* the divorce. If Taline brought him here on purpose..."

They gazed at each other. "What are the chances she *didn't* bring him here on purpose?"

"I'd say slim to no fricking way." Kai grabbed Jovan's hand. "Let's go."

When Kai opened the hall doors, the noise hit him like a tidal wave, followed closely by the stench of decay. He coughed. "What's that smell?"

Jovan's mouth was set in a grim line. "Uncle Snorre. He's forgotten his anti-odor charms again." Jovan patted his pocket. "But don't worry. I always pack extras when he's on the guest list." Jovan scanned the crowd. "I'd better catch him before he puts everyone off the food." He glanced back at Kai with a half-smile, jerking his head toward the buffet table. "I think the EO Chef is already having issues with it."

Half the guests—Radka's half—were all shorter than Kai, but Ole's half dwarfed him, even the ones who were actual dwarves. Nevertheless, Kai spotted the white chef's toque bobbing over the guests' heads, as well as at least three flailing arms. This time, Chef wasn't holding anything as innocuous as a cheese grater. The glint of silver in one massive paw wasn't a sword or an ax...

"But I bet he could still do plenty of damage with a silver cake server," Kai muttered.

"There he is," Jovan said, and plunged through the crowd.

"Jovan! Wait!" Kai reached for him, but grabbed nothing but air. He glanced around him wildly, waiting for another shriek, but nobody seemed to be paying any attention to him at all.

Shit, I know I can be unobtrusive, but this is ridiculous. He glanced down at his clothing. The EO staff's navy trousers were almost as dark as his black jeans, and his blazer was nearly the same color as theirs. *Hunh.*

Guess there's more than one way to be invisible. Most of these guests were experts in ignoring "the help." Kai might as well take advantage of it.

He knew who he needed to confront, but without Jovan at his side, he wasn't exactly the most intimidating of men. Then, amid the shifting throng in their glittering finery, he glimpsed the same Ice Pink bridesmaid who'd walked in on him and Jovan—what the heck was her name, anyway? It hardly mattered, but what she held in her hand, dangling by its tail, certainly did.

A dead rat.

Was that what she'd been looking for in the broom cupboard when she'd been supposedly looking for Ole? Surely a magical construct that had only been in existence for less than a week wouldn't have had time to attract a significant rodent population. But then he remembered what a building inspector friend had once told him. *"In any given city, you're never more than ten feet from a rat."* Apparently that applied to the Interstices too.

Ice Pink—suddenly Kai remembered her name. *Biserka.*

"A little too on the nose, if you ask me," he muttered as he dodged his way through the guests. He reached her just as she was about to lift a silver cover off a tray on the buffet table and tapped her on the shoulder. "I wouldn't do that if I were you."

Biserka glanced over her shoulder, eyes widening when she saw him. She glanced from the rat in her hand to the platter of glossy, dill-sprinkled gravlax. *Seriously? She's* still *planning to go through with it?*

Kai grabbed her wrist. "In case you haven't noticed, nobody else is paying any attention to me." He grinned evilly. "You may be the only one who can see me. And you know what that means."

She uttered a strangled shriek, which was masked by the cacophony of agitated guest chatter, Chef's anguished roars, and the scrape of Knut's violin.

"Now, take your...friend"—Kai nodded at the rat—"and get out."

She clutched the rat to her stomach—*ew!*—and bolted for the door, narrowly missing Ole's cousin Solveig, who was surveying the chaos with a huge grin.

Kai didn't even want to think about why a Valkyrie would have such a satisfied look on her face. Was she visualizing who she'd be hauling up to Valhalla before the day was over?

Kai shuddered. *Don't think about it.* But now that he had his weapon at the ready—his own visible presence—he squared his shoulders and marched toward the sound of Knut's violin. The out-of-tune notes came from over near one of the floor-to-ceiling windows—probably the only one with the drapes open, given Baba Lenka's certainty that *propuh* could infiltrate the tightest weather seals.

Ugh. The continued screeching set his teeth on edge. This was the famous performer? The incomparable, world-renowned Knut-who-needs-no-last-name? This guy's reputation was clearly overrated. As Kai neared the window, Jovan joined him once again.

"Got it sorted."

"Did Uncle Snorre really forget his charms?"

Jovan looked disgusted. "No. Imagine my surprise when he told me Taline had given him a new spell that she swore would complement the menu." He sniffed the air. "The funk is already clearing. I can smell meatballs instead of rotting flesh now."

Kai wrinkled his nose. "Lovely. By the way, I just caught Biserka—"

"Who?"

"The bridesmaid in pink who walked in on us."

"Name's a little on the nose," Jovan said with a revolted look.

"That's exactly what I said! She was about to toss a dead rat in the gravlax."

"'About to?' Didn't she succeed?"

Kai grinned and puffed out his chest a little. "Nope. I threatened her with, well, me."

Jovan lifted an eyebrow. "With you?"

"With my visibility."

Jovan laughed. "Nice one, babe." He dropped a kiss on Kai's lips, but jerked back at another screech of Knut's violin. "Loki's balls, we need to make that stop."

"On my way." He held out a hand. "Join me? Knut's never heard of me, so my presence might not convey enough of a threat. You, however?" He waggled his eyebrows and was rewarded with another of Jovan's deep, rumbly laughs. "He'll piss his pants."

"Lead the way."

With Jovan to act as juggernaut again, they reached Knut with no trouble. The violinist was standing knee deep in the marble bath full of water and drew his bow across his instrument with a teeth-gritting sound like a tortured wyvern.

"Blast! It's no good without the goat's blood." He splashed to the edge of the bath and glared at Kai. "You! You can't expect me to play under these conditions. I told your colleague that the goat sacrifice was non-negotiable."

Kai merely gazed at him, his expression bland. "I don't work for Enchanted Occasions."

Knut looked him up and down. "Then I question your...sartorial choices."

"My name," Kai leaned forward and lowered his voice to a stage whisper, "is Kai Schiffer."

Knut sniffed. "That name means nothing to me."

"No? Then perhaps you know my employer. Station KLV."

Knut's eyes widened. "You... You know that *witch*."

"I know the *bride*. She's my best friend. Oh, and by the way, I'm half Klabautermann." He wiggled his eyebrows. "And you know what *that* means." At Knut's widened eyes, Kai was tempted to add *Bwahahahahaha*, but that would be overkill. Particularly since in Knut's efforts to get as far away from Kai as possible, his feet flew out from under him and he ass-planted in the pool along with his violin.

"My Stradivarius!" he shrieked as he floundered in the water. "You've destroyed my instrument."

"I'm pretty sure you were doing a good job of that on your own," Jovan said, "judging by the sounds it was making."

"That wasn't my fault. The goat—"

"Radka! Darling!" The drapes on the next window started writhing. "I've come for you!"

Kai shared a horrified glance with Jovan. "Torvald? I thought Chef had him trapped in the fridge."

"I think Chef has other things on his mind at the moment." Jovan jerked his head toward the dais across the room where the ten-tiered wedding cake sat in pride of place atop a white-clothed table. Chef stood beside it, in goblin berserker battle stance, waving the cake server in one huge paw, a lemon juicer in the second, and a piping bag in the third, while he seemed to be throttling a dark elf with the fourth.

"Radka? Darling?" Torvald was still batting at the drapes.

"Loki's balls," Jovan muttered, "hasn't this asshole ever heard of *doors*?"

"Torvald was always about the dramatic entrance," Kai said.

"Torvald? Did you say Torvald?" Knut sloshed to his feet, his violin clutched to his chest. "Where—" He sucked in a breath as Torvald finally managed to fight free of the velvet and fling the drapes aside, the tall window backlighting him like the conquering hero who arrives in the nick of time.

"No dastardly miscreants could keep me from your side!" Torvald proclaimed, one hand pressed to his over-decorated chest. "I've come to...to..." He seemed to realize he hadn't arrived during a wedding ceremony but during what looked like a rave for unimaginative and ill-behaved cosplayers. "Radka?"

"You!" Knut bellowed.

Torvald spun to face him. "Knut?" He glanced around wildly, his blond hair flying. "This isn't what it looks like."

Jovan leaned down and murmured in Kai's ear. "This oughta be good."

Knut howled like a rabid werewolf and hurled his violin straight at Torvald's head. Torvald, who didn't lack for faults but didn't number a lack of self-preservation among them, ducked. The violin hit the window like a glass-seeking missile, shattering both.

"Damn," Jovan said admiringly. "That guy's got an arm."

Kai winced. "But I doubt he's got a Stradivarius anymore."

Knut didn't seem to care. He launched himself out of the pool and tackled Torvald. The two of them rolled on the ground in a riot of hair-pulling and name-calling, knocking several slower-moving guests off their feet.

Kai bit his lip. "Do you suppose we should intervene?"

"It would be the right thing to do," Jovan said slowly. "I suppose—"

"*Propuh!*" Baba Lenka shrieked. She clambered up on the buffet table, knocking a platter of lutefisk off onto the floor and earning an anguished howl from Chef, who waded through the crowd on a mission to rescue his creations.

"Oh, crap," Kai moaned. "Now we're in for it. Help me close the fricking drapes before we're all smothered by lousy knitting."

Kai dodged a dwarf with an elaborately braided beard who was chowing down on what looked like an entire haunch of venison while watching Knut and Torvald's continued wrestling match with detached interest, and grabbed the heavy velvet curtain. "Jovan, help me, I can't—"

Another shriek from Baba Lenka made Kai whirl.

She was no longer standing amid the meatballs and savory cheeses. She was struggling in Uncle Snorre's hands as he raised her arm to his gaping jaws.

CHAPTER TEN

"Fuck! Snorre, no!" Jovan dove through the crowd, none of whom were doing anything at all to prevent the disaster. He leaped over Knut and Torvald, then dodged around one of the interchangeable blond bridesmaids, only to find his way blocked by Chef, who hadn't been able to prevent some of the more volatile guests—which at this point was all of them—from launching an epic food fight.

The air was full of flying meatballs, fried herring, and the occasional blob of lingonberry jam.

"The Kanelsnegl!" Chef wailed. "The smørrebrød!"

Jovan detoured around his flailing arms and reached Uncle Snorre, who was peering at the shrieking Baba Lenka with a perplexed expression.

Snorre blinked at Jovan. "Ah. Jovan. I'm not impressed with the catering. This tartare doesn't seem very fresh." He poked Baba Lenka's skinny arm. "Or well-marbled."

"She's not part of the buffet, Snorre. She's the bride's grandmother." Jovan removed Baba Lenka from Snorre's arms, earning a whack on the ear for his trouble, and set her on her feet.

"Oh." Snorre nodded sagely. "That would explain it."

For her part, Baba Lenka didn't seem very grateful for the rescue. She picked up a plate of potato dumplings and threw it—not at Snorre, but at Jovan. He didn't quite manage to dodge in time—she caught his shoulder with the edge of the plate, sending it spinning to crash onto the floor at Chef's feet.

Chef's eyes glowed red and Jovan braced himself to leap between the big guy and Baba Lenka. Goblin berserkers were higher up the destructive food chain than Úlfheðinn—their tusks, not to mention the extra pair of arms, gave them a distinct advantage.

But Chef didn't go for Baba Lenka or anybody else. Instead, he lunged for a three-tiered china tea stand loaded with lacy butter cookies. He snatched it just before Baba Lenka climbed atop the table again. Given the look on his face, Jovan suspected that he'd just sighed with relief, although he couldn't hear it amid the shouts and squeals of the other guests, not to mention the further invective from Knut and Torvald, who were still rolling around on the floor. The ongoing food fight had liberally blotched Torvald's glittering doublet with gravy, jam, and —judging from the smell—pickled herring, and Knut was still leaving wet streaks on the floor.

"Loki's balls," Jovan muttered. "If this was what Kai's visibility was registering..." *Kai.* Jovan had lost sight of him in his rush to save Baba Lenka from turning into a cranky hors d'oeuvres for Uncle Snorre. He craned his neck to see over the crowd just as Ole's cousin Sven, the tallest in the family, grabbed the cookie stand in Chef's arms to keep himself from falling and sent everything— himself, cookies, tray, and Chef—crashing to the ground in a litter of broken china and buttery crumbs.

And *damn*, those two covered a *lot* of real estate.

But with the reduction in flailing arms, Jovan was able to spot Kai, who'd finally managed to close the drapes over the broken window.

Chef rose from the floor like a phoenix from the ashes— or in this case, from the buffet remains—his whites smeared with sauces, coated with crumbs, and splattered with a brighter red that looked like blood but that Jovan really hoped was lingonberry jam. "I demand satisfaction! Respect! Order! I demand—" An almond tart hit him right in the snout.

"Fuck this," Jovan growled. He charged through the crowd, glaring at everybody who dared get between him and Kai. He reached him just in time to pull him out of the way of an errant meatball. "Come on. We need to get out of here."

Kai scanned the room with wide-eyed horror, but suddenly his expression hardened and his eyes narrowed. "Taline."

"What?"

Kai jerked his head toward the hall doors. "Look at her."

So Jovan looked. The poisonous woman had a wide, satisfied grin on her face as she surveyed the chaos. "She planned all this?"

"I don't think she could have counted on Uncle Snorre snacking on Baba Lenka, but we know what she's tried to pull on poor Ole. The question is why?" Kai asked, his tone bewildered. "Radka is supposed to be her friend."

Jovan gazed down at Kai. He had flecks of chocolate dotting his glasses and a splotch of tomato sauce on his blazer sleeve, but the sight of him, the *feel* of him tucked up against Jovan's side, made his heart sing. *Anything. I'll do anything for him.* "Let's go ask her." He kissed the top of Kai's head. "I think between the ILE's infamous Beast and…well…you, we ought to be able to get her to spill."

The expression on Kai's face would have scared a confession out of a gargoyle. "Bring it."

Jovan took Kai's hand and bulled his way back into the throng. But before they got halfway across the room, a low chant raised the hair on Jovan's neck. "What the…" The air around them began to stir, the drapes billowing, the cloths on the tables whipping in the rising wind. "Fuck. Are we gonna hear about *propuh* again?"

Kai shook his head, eyes wide. "This isn't *propuh*."

"Then what—"

Atop the buffet table, Baba Lenka had raised her arms, her chant growing in speed and volume. She unwound one of her many scarves and whipped it over her head like a lasso, and the faster it moved, the stronger the wind whirling around the room.

Jovan pulled Kai against him. "Baba Lenka's doing this?"

Kai nodded. "She's a weather-worker, just like Radka and the rest of her female relatives."

He ducked as a centerpiece flew past his head and smashed against the wall. "She's terrified of a little draft and she does *this*?"

"It makes a certain sense if you think of it." Kai crouched and pulled Jovan toward the door through flying hats and whipping skirts and coattails. "She's all about controlling the wind. *Propuh* is a threat to her authority."

"Seems like overkill to me."

"Nobody ever said she was logical." Kai reached the doorway. "Taline!" he called in a voice like ice and steel. "Are you responsible for this?"

She didn't tear her gaze from the chaos, and since Baba Lenka's whirlwind was picking up speed—and cutlery— the red splatter on the walls probably wasn't entirely lingonberry-based. "It's better than I could have hoped."

"Why?" Kai demanded. "Radka is your friend."

"Yes," she said, giggling when a tureen of pea soup hit the drapes. "Which is why I know she'll forgive me once a little time has passed." A waterspout rose from Knut's abandoned marble pool. "Oooh. I've got to remember that effect."

Kai shared a mystified glance with Jovan. "So your intention wasn't to break up the wedding?"

She waved one hand. She still hadn't turned to face Kai —probably because she was used to his disembodied voice. "That was just a bonus. No, once I heard Radka hired Enchanted Occasions, I knew this was my chance. They're the only serious competition in the Interstitial wedding planning space. Discredit them, and my *own* business will be only game in town."

"So let me get this straight." Kai moved from Jovan's side to stand in front of her, and Jovan was gratified to hear her gasp. "You did all this—tortured poor Ole, planned to humiliate him in front of his friends and family, threatened Radka's happiness and peace of mind —for a *business opportunity*?"

Her mouth opened and closed like a beached carp's. "I —I—"

Kai's smile was pure evil, and Jovan was so proud he could have burst. "That's right, Taline. I'm visible. To you."

"Th-that's because the wedding is sinking. Just like I p-planned."

"You really think that's true?" Kai said, low and threatening, and Jovan's cock made a break for his fly. "Nobody else is paying any attention to me. Maybe it's *your* plans that are scuttled."

She began to back away. "It's not. You're not here for me. You can't be. I—"

Knut and Torvald collided with her legs and she went over backwards with a satisfying splat, her hands skidding in a puddle of whipped cream and fried pork belly. Jovan yanked Kai out of the path so the boneheaded idiots didn't toss him ass over tin cup as well.

However, that meant that the two of them crashed into one leg of the table holding the wedding cake. It started to tilt, Chef roaring and trying to keep the cake from falling without actually touching it, but the whole ten-tiered, buttercream-rosetted fantasy began to topple as though in slow motion.

Suddenly, his speed more startling because of the slow tumble of the cake, Andy darted into the room, muttering, "Not a person. Not a person."

Somehow, the uppermost tier, along with its vila and frost goblin topper, detached from the rest of the cake and plopped into Andy's hands without a frosting rose out of place, just as the rest of the cake smashed to the floor in a mangled mass of buttercream, lemon filling, and vanilla sponge.

Chef dropped to his knees, tears streaming down his face, his claws scraping through the mess as if he could put it back together again.

Andy peered down at him, wincing, then jerked his head at Jovan and Kai to precede him out the doors.

They'd barely made it into the entry when Solveig dashed up to them, brandishing her sword. "Leaving so soon?" She grinned, hard and bright. "Things are just getting interesting."

"Solveig," Jovan said in his best ILE agent voice, "you'd better not be planning anything that'll make me haul you into headquarters."

She paused on the threshold. "Just having a bit of fun, Jo. Don't worry. I won't inflict any *lasting* damage. I've already met my Valhalla quota for the month."

She vanished into the fray, her cry of "Hojotoho! Heiaha-ha!" ringing above the howl of the wind and Chef's cake lamentation.

Mikos, his jaw set, strode past them and pulled the doors shut with a final-sounding crash.

Andy took a deep breath and handed the cake to Kai. "Here. At least Ole and Radka can have a little of their wedding cake."

Jovan glanced around. "Where are they?" His belly filled with ice. "They're not inside, are they?"

"No. They're waiting by the intergate." He glanced over his shoulder at the doors and grimaced. "It's probably best if you join them quickly, before Mikos starts to sing. You don't want to get caught up in that."

Jovan frowned. "You want us to take them to Jotunheim?"

"No. Earthside. Las Vegas. Keep them away from both their families for a while."

"But Ole's a Pure."

"Smith configured an interface talisman just for him. He'll be fine." He turned to Kai. "You live in Earthside Vegas, right?"

"Yes." Kai drew out the word.

"Then take them to the Chapel of Elvis or something. Get them married. Have some cake." He straightened his blazer. "That's all the two of them want, right? To get married? To be happy? At Enchanted Occasions, satisfaction is *always* guaranteed."

He marched back into the banquet hall like he was going to his execution—and given the shitstorm going on behind those doors, that might not be too wide of the mark.

Jovan huffed. "How the fuck are we supposed to hide a frost goblin Earthside? Ole's not exactly an unobtrusive guy."

Kai bit his lip, brow wrinkled in a frown. But then his smile dawned, a decided twinkle in his eyes, and Jovan wanted to haul him back to that broom cupboard right the fuck now. But they'd made a vow, damn it. Ole and Radka came first.

"I've got an idea," Kai said. He spotted Brooke racing down the stairs and handed the cake top to Jovan. "Hold this for a minute?"

"Uh, sure?"

Kai raced away and caught Brooke before she could barrel across the marble floor to the banquet hall. Whatever he said to her made her glance at the hall doors uncertainly, but she nodded.

Kai beckoned to Jovan. "Come on." His grin was brighter than the chandelier. "We've got a happy ever after to facilitate."

CHAPTER ELEVEN

"I'm still not sure how we collected all these...guests."

Kai grinned at Jovan, who was sitting beside him in the Force of Love Wedding Chapel, Earthside Vegas's finest fandom-friendly quickie wedding venue. Jovan was scowling behind him at the rows of chairs, all facsimiles of the seat in the *Millennium Falcon* gun turret, and all filled with a cross section of storm troopers, Jedi knights, Darth Vaders, and Mandalorians with attendant Baby Yodas.

"I told you. The FanFunCon is in full swing, and the Star Wars fandom is heavily represented."

"Yeah, but none of them know Ole and Radka."

Kai chuckled. "You'd be surprised how many people ship Princess Leia and Chewbacca. This is probably a dream come true for them." His heart squeezed as Radka walked down the abbreviated aisle, so happy she practically glowed, and looking every inch a princess— Princess Leia to be exact, thanks to the EO stylist's quick dye spell. Radka, however, had put her foot down about the cinnamon roll hairdo, insisting on the more regal one that matched her gown. And if her long white skirts fluttered in a very localized breeze? Kai doubted any of the cosplayers who'd followed them like a gaggle of geeky ducklings noticed.

She reached the altar—or rather, the bridge—where Ole stood, the officiant next to him in full Han Solo garb, complete with Harrison Ford smirk.

Officiant Han launched into his spiel with, "A long time ago, in a galaxy far, far away."

Jovan snorted. "More appropriate than they know." He leaned over and murmured, "Ole's bandolier is a nice touch. Where'd you get it?"

"One of the Chewbaccas lent it to him." Jovan's arm settled across Kai's shoulders. *I wish it didn't feel so right there.* "Since his fur came in auburn instead of silver, I figured we should take advantage of the resemblance." Ole had informed them that his silver fur was his winter coat, and he wouldn't change color until he spent more time in Niflheim.

"At least Ole's not naked again. Technically."

Kai smothered a laugh. Because Ole—now fully refurred—was in fact wearing nothing *but* the bandolier. "We wanted him to pass Earthside, and this is the best way for him to blend in. Radka encouraged him." He nudged Jovan with his elbow. "Do you see the extremely suggestive looks she keeps giving him from under her lashes?"

"Hard to miss. Luckily Ole's too nervous to have the... reaction that would reveal he's not wearing anything but his birthday suit."

"Shhh. I want to hear their vows."

Jovan's mouth lifted in a half smile, probably because he wasn't used to being shushed. But he tucked Kai closer, and they listened to Radka and Ole promise to love each other to infinity and beyond—because apparently

Officiant Han wasn't opposed to mixing his fandom references.

When he pronounced them married, everyone stood up and cheered. They gathered around Ole and Radka, shaking hands, kissing cheeks, and slapping backs.

"Please follow me into the Mos Eisley Cantina for a toast," Officiant Han called.

Everybody boiled out of the chapel into the "cantina." Kai held back, because that last little thing—the toast—meant that it would all be over. With Radka and Ole married, their own vow was fulfilled, and that meant his time with Jovan was coming to an end.

He wanted to glom on to Jovan, never let him go. But that couldn't work. As soon as EO's interface talisman expired, Jovan would be forced to leave, and the next time Kai saw him...well...he wouldn't see Kai.

But if this was the end of their sometimes less than idyllic interlude, Kai refused to be *clingy*. Because they'd still be friends, falling back into their once-a-month get-togethers with Radka and Ole. *That'll be enough. It has to be.*

Kai laughed a little desperately. "Good thing we stashed the cake top in the hotel. It wouldn't have been enough for this crowd unless we cut the thing with a mandoline." He started for the cantina door, but Jovan caught his arm.

"Kai. Can we talk for a minute?"

Kai bit his lip, completely unable to meet Jovan's eyes. "It's okay. You don't need to say anything. We agreed. Just for the weekend. Just to get Ole and Radka their happy ever after."

"If that's what you still believe," Jovan said, in his growliest growl, "you haven't listened to anything I've said."

"I listen!" Kai protested. "You told me that we couldn't expect a repeat. That you've got your life and I've got mine. No promises. But we'll still be friends." He lifted his chin, willing it not to tremble. "See?"

"Very impressive. But one or two things have happened since then." Jovan framed Kai's face and angled it so Kai had to look at him. "Psychopathic bridesmaids. Indoor whirlwinds. Epic food fights. But you're forgetting the most important one."

"That we kept our promise to see Ole and Radka get their happy ever after?"

"No." Jovan kissed Kai, slow, soft, and sweet. "That I love you."

Kai blinked, his heart thumping loud in his ears. "Oh. That."

"And if I remember correctly"—Jovan's eyes narrowed, paralyzing Kai as effectively as a basilisk's stare—"you said you love me too."

"I... I do."

"Then what makes you think I'm willing to let you walk away now?"

Kai rested his hands on Jovan's chest. "Because you have to. I live Earthside. You live in Jotunheim. You work for an agency that enforces the separation between realms. Once that fancy talisman wears off, you won't be able to pass the Earthside intergates, and every time I come into the Interstices, I'll be invisible again. We can't—"

"Kai. I say this with the utmost love." He gazed into Kai's eyes. "Shut. Up." Kai clamped his lips together. "Good." Jovan took a deep breath and glanced around the room. His gaze landed on the chapel-provided complementary guest book, embossed with the symbol of the Rebel Alliance, and he let go of Kai. He strode across the room and flipped through the little leather-bound book to rip a page out of the back.

"Jovan! That's Ole and Radka's!"

"Yes, and it's been signed by five Obi-Wans, three Lukes, seven Reys, and an assortment of storm trooper IDs. I don't think it'll have quite the sentimental value you imagine. Besides..." He flapped the little paper. "This is blank." He grabbed a pen shaped like a light saber and returned to Kai's side. "Now, I'm going to say something, and after I do, I'm not going to be able to speak again for twenty-four hours. And after that, I'll probably be hauled in to ILE headquarters and subjected to interrogation by a panel of extremely humorless IA drones."

"You... Why? You haven't done anything. They can't hold you responsible for the wedding carnage, can they?"

"No, although I suspect the ILE will be called in to investigate. No, this is because I'm about to break one of my ILE vows, and those are enforced magically. Kai, I'm —"

Kai clapped a hand over Jovan's mouth. "Don't. If whatever it is will get you in trouble, just don't. We'll always be friends. We just won't be able to be together." Kai's voice broke. *Damn it, I'm* trying *to be strong here.*

Jovan grasped Kai's wrist and gently freed his mouth. "That's not enough for me. I love you. I want the same kind of future with you that Ole and Radka have ahead of them. I'm not willing to settle for less." His expression turned anxious. "That is, if you want that too."

"I want nothing more. But we *can't.* We—"

"I'm an aitcher." Jovan grimaced, clenching his eyes shut as if he were bracing for a blow.

Kai gaped at him. "What?"

Jovan cracked one eye open. "I—" Both eyes popped wide. "I can still speak."

Kai planted his fists on his hips. "Yes, and you'd better start talking *now*."

Jovan whooped, a grin splitting his face. He grabbed Kai around the waist and whirled him in a crazy dance. "I can *speak*."

"Jovan. I'm getting dizzy. Please stop and tell me what's going on."

He did, but kept Kai wrapped tight in his arms. *Totally okay*. "I'm an aitcher. My mother was Angrboða. You already know my father wasn't Loki, but he wasn't another Jötunn the way everyone assumes. He was human."

"But why keep it a secret?"

Jovan smoothed Kai's hair off his forehead. "You more than anyone know the average Pure's attitude toward aitchers. In fact, the ILE doesn't normally employ aitchers at all because most of the top brass have the same attitude. The ILE can't afford for their agents' authority and effectiveness to be compromised by anti-aitcher bias." He shrugged. "So our vows prevent us from spilling."

"But—"

"If we reveal any information that puts the agency in danger, we activate a spell that mutes us for a full day." He smiled down at Kai. "But if I can speak after I confessed my nature to you, then the spell must recognize that my position, my work, the agency itself, isn't compromised by you knowing. In fact"—his eyes glinted with humor, something most people would never expect from Jovan Kos—"how committed are you to your job at the TV station now that Radka won't be there anymore?"

Kai's head was still reeling from Jovan's revelation. "I— What?"

"How would you feel about working for the ILE? We could use someone with your abilities." He waggled his eyebrows. "Covert intelligence."

Kai snorted. "Right. Until something went wrong and I popped into view at exactly the wrong time."

"Even that might work well. You wielded your visibility the way I wield my wolf rage. But there are ways to serve other than in the field. You're a problem solver. The ILE needs problem solvers, because in case you haven't noticed, the adversarial relationships between realms, between races, haven't eased in the last couple of millennia."

Kai bit his lip. "I don't know…"

"You don't have to decide right now. I just want to throw it out there as an option. Something to think about while we decide where we want to live."

Kai had to force himself to *breathe*. "Where we— You mean together?"

Jovan nodded. "That's my idea of a happy ever after." His smile turned almost shy. "What do you say? Want to take our own turn here in the Force of Love Chapel?" He kissed Kai again. "I hear they serve a mean toast in the cantina. And the souvenir guest book is a bonus." He scrunched his face up. "I know I'm not the best bet. You could do better. I mean, I'm the Beast."

Kai cupped Jovan's cheek, relishing the brush of scruff under his palm. "Not to me. Never to me. And never to

Ole or Radka either. If you're a beast, then you're the best beast in the world. And if I'm lucky…" He bit his lip.

"Don't stop now."

"If I'm lucky, you're *my* beast."

"Baby, I've been your beast since the first moment I didn't see you." He kissed Kai again, heat building between them that the Chapel's air conditioning couldn't dissipate. "And I want to not see you again every day for the rest of our lives. What do you say?"

Kai grinned. "I'd say…" He snugged his hips against Jovan's. "I'd say…" He rose on his tiptoes and nipped Jovan's earlobe. "I'd say…" He kissed Jovan's eyebrow, cheekbone, jaw, *mouth*. "*Rawr*."

Don't miss the other Enchanted Occasions stories,
beginning with *Nudging Fate!*

ABOUT

With his heart's desire at stake, can he resist giving Fate a little nudge?

Half-norn event planner Anders Skuldsson is under strict orders from Asgard not to meddle with Fate. But with Enchanted Occasions' latest booking—the competition for the hand of Faerie's one true prince—crashing around his ears, it's really, really, *really* difficult to toe that particular line. So if Andy just *happens* to pose as a contender for the prince? It's an *emergency*, damn it. Besides, it's only temporary, so Odin can hardly blame him. Right?

If Conall of Odstone hadn't sworn a blood oath to protect his half-brother, Prince Reyner, he'd murder the idiot himself. Rey was supposed to be here, choosing a mate before being crowned and wed. Instead, he'd left Con to impersonate him. Again.

But when Con meets Andy, his anger turns to desire… and despair. Even if Andy forgives him for pretending to be someone he's not, how could a man as appealing and accomplished as Andy—a man who's eligible for a prince's hand, for pity's sake—settle for the court outcast?

As for Andy, his burgeoning feelings for the prince are both unfortunate and hopeless because *hello*? Half-norn? Faerie prince? Not exactly a match made in Valhalla.

When the Faerie Queen herself hands down an ultimatum, their double-deception isn't their only obstacle. Unless Andy makes the right decision, both their fates could be sealed by... well... Fate.

a message from
❧ *ej*

Dear Reader,

Thank you so much for reading *Best Beast*, the introduction to my Enchanted Occasions story world. I'm so happy you've taken this journey with me! I'd be immensely grateful if you'd take a moment to leave a review at the retailer and any other site you use for reviews. Believe me, reviews make an *enormous* difference to the health and well-being of books (and not incidentally, to their associated authors!).

Wondering what to read next? If you haven't caught the EO team's other adventures, be sure to check out *Nudging Fate* and *Devouring Flame*. If you're a fan of contemporary romance, you might like *Clickbait*, where love blossoms at a construction site, between a prickly web designer and a family-focused electrician. If you're in the mood for something a little less, er, reality-based, there's my Mythmatched story universe—paranormal romantic comedy, beginning with *Cutie and the Beast*, where a cursed fae warrior turned psychologist clashes with his determined temporary office manager. As you might expect, hi-jinks ensue!

Pop on over to my website, https://ejrussell.com, for all the deets on my books—my paranormal rom-coms and mysteries, my contemporary romances, and my one lone historical. If you're an audio fan, you can find the audio scoop there too. *Best Beast*, for instance, is narrated by the wonderful Kirt Graves. (The QR code below will get you there with your smartphone camera or other code reader.)

Would you like exclusive content and ARC giveaways, not to mention gratuitous dance videos? Then I'd love for you to join me in E.J. Russell's Reality Optional, my Facebook fan group (https://facebook.com/groups/reality.optional). My newsletter is the place to get the latest dish on new releases, sales, and more. I promise I only send one out when I've got…well…news. You can subscribe here: https://ejrussell.com/newsletter.

All my best,
—E

Also by
ej

Paranormal Romance
Mythmatched Universe
Fae Out of Water Trilogy
Cutie and the Beast
The Druid Next Door
Bad Boy's Bard

Supernatural Selection Trilogy
Single White Incubus
Vampire With Benefits
Demon on the Down-Low

Other Mythmatched Romances
Howling on Hold
Possession in Session
Witch Under Wraps
Cursed is the Worst
The Skinny on Djinni
Assassin by Accident (part of Carnival of Mysteries)

Quest Investigations Mysteries
Five Dead Herrings
The Hound of the Burgervilles
The Lady Under the Lake
Death on Denial

At Odds with the Gods (A Mythmatched / Purgatory Playhouse crossover)

Mythmatchedlets (Mythmatched companion stories, free to newsletter subscribers in ebook form, collected in one paperback volume: *Second First Date, Rusty's Really Bad Day, First Flight, Getting the Band Together, Purgatory Postscript, A Very Quest Solstice*)

Magic Emporium Series (shared world)
Purgatory Playhouse

Enchanted Occasions Series
Best Beast
Nudging Fate
Devouring Flame

Ghost Townies Series
Ghostridden

Legend Tripping Series
Stumptown Spirits
Wolf's Clothing

Art Medium Series
The Artist's Touch
Tested in Fire
Art Medium: The Complete Collection (omnibus edition)

Royal Powers Series (shared world)
Duking It Out

Duke the Hall
King's Ex

Science Fiction
Sun, Moon, and Stars Series
Partnership
Principles

Interdimensional Time Bureau
Monster Till Midnight

Historical Romance
Silent Sin

Contemporary Romance
Camera Shy
Summer Kitchen
The Thomas Flair
Mystic Man
For a Good Time, Call… (A Bluewater Bay novel, with
Anne Tenino)

Christmas Kisses (holiday shorts)
The Probability of Mistletoe
An Everyday Hero
A Swants Soiree

Geeklandia Series
The Boyfriend Algorithm (M/F)
Clickbait

Writing as Nelle Heran
(traditional cozy mystery)

Crafty Sleuth Series (with C.K. Eastland)
Die Cut
Mixed Media
Found Objects (*coming soon*)

About the
Author

E.J. Russell (she/her), author of the award-winning Mythmatched paranormal romance series, writes LGBTQ+ romance and mystery in a rainbow of flavors. Count on high snark, low angst, and happy endings.

Reality? Eh, not so much.

She's married to Curmudgeonly Husband, a man who cares even less about sports than she does. Luckily, C.H. also loves to cook, or all three of their children (Lovely Daughter and Darling Sons A and B) would have survived on nothing but Cheerios, beef jerky, and Satsuma mandarins (the extent of E.J.'s culinary skill set).

E.J. also writes traditional cozy mystery as Nelle Heran. She lives in rural Oregon, enjoys visits from her wonderful adult children, and indulges in good books, red wine, and the occasional hyperbole.

News & Social Media:
Website: https://ejrussell.com
Newsletter: https://ejrussell.com/newsletter

Acknowledgements

I owe many thanks to the wonderful Kim Fielding, who sent me the link to an article about *propuh*. It sent this story in a completely different direction than I originally imagined—and a much better one, I think! Thanks also to Lucy Lennox for her kindness, generosity, and support in creating an opportunity for so many authors to share their stories with new readers.

Thank you to Natasha Snow for the cover design concept, Meg DesCamp for editing and encouragement (aka browbeating), and NOLAKim for assistance and moral support.

Thanks to my family—Jim, Hana, Nick, Ross, and Billy —for not rolling their eyes when I say, "I've got a book releasing today!" Love you, guys!

And, always and forever, thank you to my readers for accompanying me on this journey. You're the reason I can continue to follow my heart, and I appreciate you more than I can say.